Rebel Horse Rescue

Horses and Friends Series

Rebel Horse Rescue
Horses and Friends 5

By

Miralee Ferrell

Rebel Horse Rescue
Published by Mountain Brook Ink
White Salmon, WA U.S.A.

The website addresses shown in this book are not intended in any way to be or imply an endorsement on the part of Mountain Brook Ink, nor do we vouch for their content.

This book is a work of fiction. All characters and events are the product of the author's imagination. Any resemblance to any person, living or dead, is coincidental.

Scripture quotations are taken from the King James Version of the Bible. Public domain.

ISBN 978-1-943959-14-3

The Team: Miralee Ferrell, Nikki Wright, Jenny Mertes, Cindy Jackson
Cover Design: DogEared Design, Kirk DouPonce

Mountain Brook Ink is an inspirational publisher offering fiction you can believe in.
Printed in the United States of America

*To Kate, my darling granddaughter,
I hope by the time you're old enough
to read these books, you'll love horses
and reading as much as I do.*

CHAPTER ONE

Hood River, Oregon, summer, current day

KATE STOOD WITH HER FRIENDS TORI, Colt, and Melissa, and their new friend Jake, and waved at her little brother, Pete, as he climbed into the back seat of their family's Subaru. "Have a wonderful time at camp, Pete!"

Melissa stepped forward and peeked into the open window at six-year-old Pete. "I'm so glad you get to go. When you come home, I'll have a bag of M&M's for you to celebrate, okay?"

Colt tossed her a grin. "I'll do one better." He dug into the back pocket of his jeans and pulled out a rumpled brown package. "Here you go, buddy. Ask your mom and dad if it's okay for you to eat these before you scarf them all down. I know you like the ones without peanuts best."

Tori's lower lip wobbled. "I didn't get you anything. I'm sorry, Pete."

The little boy had sat with his face forward during most of the conversation, but he turned his head slightly and held out his hand. Then his gaze swung and briefly met Tori's. What appeared to be a barely noticeable smile flickered over his face.

Kate gave a soft gasp. Was it intentional or only a twitching muscle? Since her little brother was autistic, it was rare for him to meet someone's eyes. Joy rose in her spirit, and she almost rushed to the door and pulled her little brother into a hug. She walked two steps toward the car and then stopped. Pete had come a long way, especially since meeting Jake's dog, Mouse, and spending more time with Kate's group of friends. But a hug would make him retreat further into his shell, so she'd better not push it.

She settled for briefly touching his hair. He didn't flinch and pull away, but Kate saw no positive response, either. She sighed. One baby step at a time. Maybe this camp for autistic kids would help him.

Her mom placed a hand on Kate's shoulder, making her jump. "You'll remember all the things I told you? Stay at home, and no riding your bikes over to Mrs. Maynard's house."

Kate frowned. "Ah, Mom, she's expecting us today. We told her we'd help with her yard work. After she gave Tori her horse, we owe her big time. We can't let her down."

Nan Ferris raised a brow. "No, she's not. I called and told her we'd be gone a few hours, and I wanted you close to home. Mrs. Maynard understood. You can go tomorrow. It's not going to kill you to stay home." She looked from Colt's freckled face to Kate's best friend Tori's golden-hued one, to Melissa's face ringed by blonde hair, to Jake, the ever-present clown who loved to quote old TV shows and movies. "Can I trust the four of you—" She moved her stare to Kate— "the five of you, to stay out of trouble and not ride any of the horses while I'm gone? Grooming or ground work is fine. But you stay on the property and behave, or this will be the last time I leave you alone."

"We're not little kids, Mom." Kate scrubbed her toe in the loose gravel next to the car, totally embarrassed in front of her friends. "Most of us are thirteen, and Colt's almost fourteen."

Colt grinned and spit out the piece of straw he'd been chewing on. "We'll be good, Mrs. Ferris. We promise. I'll keep the rest of these guys in line. And hey, I feel pretty lucky that you trust us so much. My parents wouldn't allow five kids to be at their house alone for two hours while they were gone, especially *these* four." Jake punched him in the arm, having to reach a bit due to his much shorter stature. "Like you're a perfect angel."

Kate cleared her throat. "We'll all be perfect angels, Mom. Don't worry." At times it still shocked her that she had such a varied set of friends—she chanced a glance at Melissa, one girl she'd never have expected to be part of their group. But Melissa wasn't the same snobby rich girl she'd been when she first brought her horse here to board. She'd changed a lot since her dad left and took the family money with him, leaving Melissa and her mom in a tight spot.

"Not much chance of the five of you turning into angels, but if I didn't trust you, I wouldn't be leaving. I'll still worry until your dad and I pull back into the driveway."

Kate's dad, sitting behind the wheel of the car, broke into a soft laugh. "Come on, Nan, they're all great kids. And you're right—we can trust them not to get into trouble. You can call home every fifteen minutes if it'll make you feel better."

Nan's brows lowered. "That might be overdoing it a little, but I will call you in an hour. The camp doesn't encourage parents to stick around, since it can make the children more anxious. We'll drop Pete off and head right home."

"I know, Mom. You told us, and we visited the camp a week ago and heard all the rules, remember? You should get going or you'll be late, right?"

"Right." Her dad echoed the word and turned the key in the ignition. "Let's go, Nan. Time's a-wastin'."

Kate's mother gave another concerned look at the group, then slipped into the passenger side and closed the door. "Don't do anything I wouldn't do while we're gone. And I'll call you again when we're halfway home, so keep the phone close."

"Sure, Mom, not a problem." Kate held up the cordless from the house and gave her a serious look. "See you in a couple of hours, but no need to rush. What can possibly happen in that amount of time?"

An hour later, Kate sat on a bale of straw in the barn and stared at her friends, who were sprawled across an assortment of bales in the area where they kept the shavings and straw for the stalls. "All right, guys. We've groomed the horses, talked about what we're doing the rest of the summer—which sure isn't much—and we still have over an hour until Mom and Dad get home. Do you think we should still go to Mrs. Maynard's later?"

Tori's black ponytail swayed as she shook her head. "Nope. Your mom said she's not expecting us 'til tomorrow. I don't suppose we could visit Mr. Wallace? He's only a quarter-mile down the road. We could walk there and not ride our bikes. I'm sure he'd like company."

Colt smirked. "Mr. Wallace loves when we bring cookies, and unless I'm mistaken, you girls have been letting him down in that department." He suddenly sat up straight, his eyes gleaming. "Hey, why don't we make a big batch of cookies?"

"*We?*" Melissa sniffed. "You mean me, Kate, and Tori, right? While you and Jake sit around the kitchen and pester us to hurry so you can have the beaters and the bowl. Besides, you guys are impossible to keep out of the cookies. Most of them will be eaten before we get there."

"And Mom said not to leave the property," Kate said. "She's already called once to check on us and reminded me of that." She pulled a face. "Although I suppose we could make a double batch and take them later."

Colt grinned. "Now you're talking. What do you think, Jake? What's your favorite cookie?"

Jake rolled from his back onto his stomach and looked up. "I like any kind, but especially the ones Cookie Monster ate.

He was my favorite Sesame Street character because he loved cookies, know what I mean?"

Colt laughed. "Yeah, we gotcha, Jake. Anything with sugar. But I'm guessing we need to keep you from eating too many, or you'll be bouncing off the walls." He tossed a handful of straw at Jake.

Melissa stood and stretched, then stopped, one hand still in the air. "Listen. Did you hear that?"

"Hear what?" Kate scrunched her brows.

"Hoofbeats on the driveway. Are you expecting someone to ride over today to use the arena?"

Kate shook her head. "Nope. Someone could stop by, but most of the people who board their horses here come in a car, or ride a bike, or walk, since their horse is already in the barn. Probably someone riding by." She smiled. "We do live in horse country, you know."

A loud nicker outside was answered by two horses in the barn, and Kate swung around to face the outside door. "Better go check it out, though." Kate was certain it wouldn't amount to anything. There hadn't been any excitement around here since the theft of her mom's antique box containing the money for the trail ride and scavenger hunt. It had been quiet and boring the past couple of weeks.

The group hurried outside with Kate leading the way. She came to a quick halt a few paces from the barn and gasped. "It's a loose horse with a halter on. And he's gorgeous!"

Tori came to a sliding stop behind her and bumped her shoulder. "Oops, sorry. Hey, Jake, slow down, or you're gonna knock us all over." She shot Jake a smile. "Although I don't have the right to talk—I ran into Kate."

Colt whistled, but Melissa stood silent. Colt moved toward the horse, holding out his hand. "Hey, boy. Where did you come from?"

Jake hung back. "What color would you call him? Brown?"

Kate grinned "Well, kinda. But horse people would call him a bay."

Melissa nodded. "A black bay, actually, since he's a really rich, dark brown with black points on his legs and a black mane and tail."

"So where did he come from? Were you guys expecting him to show up and board here or something?" Jake looked from Kate to her other friends.

Colt punched Jake in the arm. "Dude, that's a crazy question, even for you. Horses don't bring themselves to a barn to be boarded—their owners bring them and fill out the paperwork."

Jake grinned. "Well, you never know. You remember Mr. Ed, the talking horse on that old TV show, right? He could have brought himself and probably even figured out a way to fill out the forms."

Colt heaved a long sigh. "I've never even seen that show, but I remember my grandmother mentioning it. How do you come up with all this stuff, Jake? Do you stay up all night watching old reruns, or what?"

Jake opened his mouth to reply but Colt held up his hand. "I know, Netflix. Now come on, let's see if we can catch this big boy. Someone's probably frantically looking for their horse and they'll turn up any minute. I'm sure they'll be glad we've got him."

Colt took a step toward the horse, but Kate grabbed his arm. "Hold it, Colt. How about we take hay into the smaller arena and leave the gate open? If he doesn't go on his own, we can chase him in. It would be simple for him to get away out here or race around in the big arena. A lot of horses are skittery around strangers, and I don't want him to spook and take off down the road."

"Good plan. I'll grab a flake of hay." Melissa disappeared into the barn.

Tori trotted toward the gate on the outdoor arena, swinging wide around the horse, now grazing along the outside of the fence. She unlatched the gate and pulled it toward her, waiting for Melissa to take the hay in and dump it on the far side.

Melissa hurried back out. "Now what? He sniffed it as I walked by, but he seems more interested in the grass."

"Yep." Kate moved toward the gelding. "Typical horse. Let's form a half-circle and move him into the arena. Jake, you can help too. Keep your arms out wide and walk slow so we don't scare him."

They spent the next few minutes herding the big bay through the open gate, then Tori grabbed the top rail and swung it shut behind him. "Are you gonna try to catch him now, Kate? See what he's like?"

Kate nodded. "I'll get a lead rope and give him a few minutes to munch. Then I'll see if we can snap the rope on him. I'll bet someone comes along before he finishes that hay and claims him."

Jake eyed the horse. "What if no one claims him? Then what?"

Colt laughed. "Not gonna happen. He's not thin, his halter is in good shape, even if he shouldn't be wearing it. It's not worn out or growing into his face, his coat is shiny, so he must have owners who care for him."

Jake made a face. "I guess I haven't been around horses long enough to get what you're saying. Why would a halter grow into his face? And why shouldn't he wear it? Horses wear halters, right? What's the big deal?"

Melissa looked at Kate and raised her brows. Kate waved a hand. "You tell him. I'm going to go in and see if I can pet him."

Jake backed up a pace. "I'm going to stay back a little. He's kind of big and scary. No offense, guys, but you know I'm not big on horses. You guys should wait until Kate's parents get back. You don't know anything about this guy."

Colt ignored him and walked beside Kate to the gate. "I'm going in with you, just in case."

"In case of what?"

He shrugged. "I dunno. In case you have any problems and need help, I guess."

Melissa waved a hand. "You want me and Tori to come too?"

Kate shook her head. "Nope. He might get spooked. Maybe you should stay on the fence rail instead."

"Okay." Melissa leaned against the top rail of the white fence. "So, it's like this, Jake. If a horse is wearing a halter for a long time and it's too tight, it can start cutting into his face and give him sores. And if it's too sloppy, he might be rubbing on a metal fence post and get the halter hung up, and hurt himself trying to get free. Lots of things can happen, and that's why it's not safe or smart to leave one on a horse that's not tied up."

Jake edged toward the fence. "So why do you think this one is wearing a halter?"

Melissa shrugged. "Maybe he's hard to catch or the owners are lazy. Hard to say. I guess we'll have to see if Kate has any trouble catching him." Melissa turned toward the center of the arena, then grinned and nudged Tori. They watched Jake moving away from the fence toward the barn. Melissa lowered her voice so only Tori could hear. "Jake's funny, and he's nice. Too bad he's scared of horses."

"Yeah, but I was kind of scared too, when I first met Kate."

"Seriously? I guess I didn't really know you then. But I can't tell it now. You do great with Starlight." She glanced at Kate, who was moving slowly toward the gelding, the rope behind her back and her other hand extended. Colt stayed a little off to the side. "Kate's smart not to rush him."

"Yeah. She's good with horses," Tori said. "She's why I got over being afraid. She helped me a lot."

Melissa gave a shy smile. "Kate has helped a lot of people. She's kind of special that way, don't you think?"

"Sure do."

Kate turned her head. "Hey, my face is turning red, you guys. I mean, I appreciate everything you're saying, but it's kind of embarrassing."

Melissa clapped a hand over her mouth. "Oops. I didn't think you were listening. Sure glad it was only nice stuff." She giggled and nudged Tori.

Kate smirked. "Now that sounds more like it. I'm not going to talk anymore. I think we probably all need to be quiet so we don't scare him, although he looks pretty happy with his nose in the hay. I'll bet he's gentle as a lamb."

Colt snorted. "I'm not so sure. While you girls have been gabbing, he's been watching you. See how he's kept his head facing you? I've seen the whites of his eyes a couple of times, like he's right on the edge of bolting. I'm not sure how close you'll get to him, Kate."

"Right. I'll move slower." She stopped about ten feet from the horse and crooned soft words, then dug into her pocket and pulled out a carrot. "Come on, boy. I have a special treat for you."

He extended his neck and his nostrils fluttered, then he gave a soft nicker and moved a step toward her. Kate halted and waited, hoping he'd come to her. She'd have to move carefully when it came time to snap on the lead, but he'd probably been handled a lot and wouldn't care. He was simply leery of strangers and the new surroundings.

The gelding took another step, his lower lip moving like he wanted to snatch the treat off her palm.

"That's right, boy. Another step or two and you can have it." She extended her arm a little more and waited.

The big horse moved cautiously toward her and halted, barely out of reach.

Colt stood completely still, but his quiet voice carried to Kate. "I think you should pull your arm back a bit, then take a step or two closer so you're within reach of his halter while he eats the carrot."

"Right. Good idea." Kate did as he suggested, and when the gelding plucked the carrot from her hand, she reached out and snapped the rope onto the ring under his chin. "I've got him!" Triumph soared through her, and she reached up to stroke the bay's face.

His eyes widened, and his head jerked up. Quickly, he backed a few steps with Kate following, then just as suddenly, he reared straight up, striking at the air.

Surprise hit Kate so hard, she almost dropped the rope. She realized what she was doing and renewed her grip, then braced herself and held on tight.

Colt stood to the side, shock covering his face. "I think you'd better let go, Kate. You're going to get struck by those front hooves. He's not wearing shoes, but he could still do a lot of damage."

At that moment Kate heard a car pull in and come to a stop behind her next to the arena. Kate didn't want to take her eyes off the horse as he continued to rear and pull against the rope, dragging her several feet across the arena. She hoped the horse's owner had come to claim him, and she could turn him over to someone who could handle him.

"Kate!" her dad's voice boomed at the same time the car door slammed. "What in the world are you doing in there with that horse? Get out of there before he kills you!"

CHAPTER TWO

KATE DIDN'T TURN HER HEAD AND kept her gaze on the rearing horse. "I can't, Dad. I don't know what he'll do if I let go." Out of the corner of her eye, she saw the gate swing open and her mother slip through. Her mom was a horse person, while her dad definitely wasn't.

Mom eased into the arena and walked slowly toward Kate, talking in a soothing, low tone to the animal. He stopped rearing but snorted and pulled back against the rope. "Kate, I want you to move with him. Don't try to hold him, or you're going to get serious rope burns on your hands. If he pulls away from you, walk that direction. I think it's scaring him more that you're fighting him, and you don't need to get dragged."

"Right." Kate did as her mother suggested the next time the gelding lunged back. "What now? Should I let the lead rope go and hope we can catch him later and take it off, or hold on and hope he calms down?"

Her mother moved another couple of paces closer to Kate, keeping her voice low. "Where's his owner, and what are you doing in here with a half-wild animal?" She shook her head. "Never mind. We'll sort it out once we decide what to do. Keep moving with him. John," she said to Kate's dad without looking that way, "would you send one of the kids after a little more hay? Maybe get a scoop of grain as well."

"I'll go." Colt moved from the fence slowly then ran after he'd gotten a couple of yards away. He was back in under two minutes with a flake of hay and some grain in a bucket. "What should I do with it?"

"Shove the hay under the bottom rail close to the horse and pour the grain on top. If he's ever had grain before, I'm guessing he'll calm down and go straight for it."

Colt did as he'd been asked then went back to stand near Jake, who was talking in soft tones to Melissa and Tori.

"Mom, he's headed for the hay." Relief hit Kate hard, and she realized for the first time that her arms were tired.

"Yes, I see. Let him settle down and eat. I'm going to come up beside you and move slowly toward him to unsnap the rope so he doesn't step on it and hurt himself." She waited for the horse to stick his nose deep into the hay and grain, then walked to him, keeping one hand on the rope. She was able to unsnap the clasp with the gelding only giving a snort and a toss of his head before he resumed eating.

All Kate's muscles seemed to turn to Jell-O at once, and she almost sank to the ground. Her mom grabbed her hand and drew Kate with her to the gate, where Dad waited to let them out, then swung it shut and securely latched it behind them.

Both of her parents turned at the same time, their eyes narrowed and mouths turned down. Her dad drew in a deep breath. "Does anyone want to tell us what's going on here? Kate, what in the world made you and Colt go into that corral and try to work with that horse? You could have been killed!"

An hour later, Kate, her parents, and her four friends sat in the living room nibbling on cookies her mom had pulled from the freezer and warmed in the microwave. Kate leaned forward, her snack forgotten, as her father hung up the phone. "What did the sheriff say?"

John Ferris took a sip of his coffee, then he gave Kate a serious look. "He doesn't have a report of the horse that showed up here being missing. But he does have a report of a gray Arabian and a chestnut Thoroughbred turning up at someone else's place."

"Huh?" Kate frowned. "What's up with that?"

"There are several horses reported missing and two or three other people who have called in with horses that showed up at their farms or houses. None of them match the description I gave him of this gelding. He asked us to take two or three photos of the horse and send it to him for his files. He's too busy to come out today, so I offered."

Tori's forehead wrinkled. "But why are so many missing? I mean, that's kind of weird, right?"

"Yeah," Kate echoed, "how could so many be loose?"

Her dad leaned back in his easy chair. "He said the people who called in to report their horses missing claim they were in a pasture with a closed gate, or in one case, kept in a stall. All he can guess is that pranksters decided it would be funny to open a few gates or stall doors." He shook his head.

Colt huffed. "That's not even a little funny. The owners must be worried."

Kate's mom nodded. "Not to mention how dangerous it is to turn a horse loose."

"You mean they're all wild like the one that came here?" Jake's eyes widened.

Kate giggled. "No, silly. But think about it. What if one goes running down the road and gets hit by a car? The horse could get killed."

He frowned. "Yeah. And the people in the car could get hurt, too. A horse is a whole lot bigger than a deer, and they can do serious damage to a car. I know because my older brother hit a deer on the way home in the dark a few weeks ago. It broke the windshield and smashed the grill on the front. Pops was not happy."

Kate's dad smiled. "I imagine not. There's also the problem of a horse trying to get into a pasture with other horses. He could get cut or tangled in wire, or get kicked—or kick one of them, breaking a leg or worse. There are all sorts of reasons you don't want horses running free."

Melissa shivered. "Besides how horrible it would be not to know where your horse was or if you'd ever get it back. Somebody could decide they want to keep it and never call the sheriff. That would be awful!"

Tori bit her lip. "I don't understand why anyone would be so mean. Like Colt said, that's not funny at all."

Kate hated what she was hearing, although she knew it could be true. How could people neglect their animals or be cruel enough to turn one loose that belonged to another person? "But, Dad, you said no one has called about the gelding we have? What does the sheriff want us to do? Can we take him somewhere and drop him off until the owners claim him?"

"I'm afraid not, honey." Her dad shot a glance at her mom. "He said they don't have the resources for that, and he asked that we keep the horse here, since we're a boarding stable. He hasn't had this happen before, so he'll have to look up the law and see how long we have to keep him until we could sell him, if no one ever turns up. That's highly unlikely, though. He's guessing the owners might not be home, and as soon as they return and discover he's missing, they'll probably call. He'll give them our address and phone number, as well as call us himself to let us know the owners are on the way."

Colt stood. "Pretty crazy, if you ask me. Let's hope it doesn't happen again, and all the owners find their horses by morning. I'd better get home. Mom and Dad will be wondering why I'm staying so long."

"Yeah, me too," Jake said. "I've got my bike, so I'll ride home."

Tori and Melissa both stood up. Tori said, "Thanks for the cookies, Mrs. Ferris. Is it okay if I come over in the morning and help Kate with chores? I need to clean Starlight's stall and exercise him, anyway."

"Sure, sounds good." Kate's mom picked up the plate of cookies and headed for the kitchen. She slowed and spoke over her shoulder, her words ending with a chuckle. "Hopefully we won't have any more runaways that show up in the night. If so, you kids might have to do some sleuthing and see if you can solve this mystery."

"Yeah, why didn't I think of that?" Kate's eyes widened, and she looked from one friend to the other. "Somebody needs to find out where this horse came from, if his owners don't show up by tomorrow. But even more than that, we need to see if we can figure out who's letting the horses out before one of them gets hurt."

CHAPTER THREE

THE NEXT DAY, KATE, TORI, COLT, and Melissa sat around the kitchen table drinking orange juice after a late breakfast. All three of her friends had come to help get chores done fast so they could investigate the strange horse. Jake had called to say his parents wanted his help with yard work at home, and he couldn't come over until later, if at all.

Kate set her glass on the table and looked from one expectant face to another, then she turned to her mother, who was finishing stacking the dishwasher. "Mom, you said you were going to call the sheriff again this morning while we finished chores in the barn. Did you get any more news? Has the owner come forward to claim our horse yet?"

Her mother wiped her hands on a dish towel. "Remember, he's not our horse. The sheriff said they had reports of three more horses loose this morning, and he's not happy. He's had several phone calls from owners who are worried sick about their horses, not to mention disgruntled people whose lawns have been torn up by stray horses grazing on their flowers and grass. And not a word from anyone on the bay gelding." She leaned a hip against the counter. "We can't keep calling him the bay gelding. Have you kids talked about a name for him?"

Colt shifted in his chair. "It does sound kind of stupid calling him the bay or that horse. You guys have any ideas?"

Melissa pursed her lips, and Tori narrowed her eyes, but neither one said anything, so Colt turned to Kate. "You always have good ideas. Anything hitting you this time?"

"Well . . ." She tipped her head to the side as a thought blossomed and grew. "He is pretty wild. I don't think he's mean or anything, it's more like he acts out because he's scared, or maybe because no one's ever really loved him. You know, kind of like kids who come from homes where they're ignored, so they rebel?"

Melissa ducked her head and gave a quick nod. "Yep. I know exactly what you're talking about."

Kate sucked in a sharp breath, suddenly sick that she'd said anything that might have hurt Melissa. "I'm so sorry. I didn't mean anything personal."

Melissa raised her head and gazed at Kate, but her eyes didn't reflect any anger, just a little sadness. "It's okay. Seriously. I totally get what you mean, and I agree."

Kate twirled a strand of her curly hair around her finger, realizing part of it had come loose from the braid she'd thrown together this morning. "I was thinking maybe we should call him Rebel or something." She looked from one face to another, then up at her mother. "Mom?"

Her mother nodded. "I like it. I think it fits. Unless someone else has a suggestion? We need to keep the floor open, then take a vote if there are more ideas."

The corner of Kate's mouth lifted. "We don't have to go with my suggestion, if you guys think of something."

Colt grinned his wide, slow grin. "Beats anything I can come up with. Melissa? Tori? How about you? And should we call Jake to see what he thinks and give him a vote? He was here when the horse showed up, and we shouldn't leave him out."

Tori thumped her fingers on the table. "Rebel. He's a rebel of a horse, and we're trying to rescue him—if he'll let us. It's kind of cool. I like it. How about you, Melissa?"

She gave a thumbs up. "Yep. Awesome name, but why don't you call Jake real quick? We shouldn't leave him out." She winced. "I know how that feels. And I don't mean with you guys. But when some of my old friends dumped me after my dad left Mom, I almost broke; it hurt something awful. If I can help it, I won't ever be mean to anyone again. Mean is definitely *not* cool."

Kate reached for the phone lying on the counter and dialed Jake's number. The room grew quiet while everyone waited for her to finish explaining to Jake.

All of a sudden, she moved the receiver away from her ear as his voice blasted into the room. "That's so awesome! Did you ever see the old black and white TV show called *The Rebel*? I think it was only on for two or three seasons, but it was in the Old West and had cowboys and outlaws and stuff. Our Rebel would fit right in."

Kate realized Jake had finished talking and moved the phone back to her ear. "Yeah. Thanks, Jake. And no, I've never seen that show. I'm guessing maybe they don't show reruns. I don't know how you find so many old shows nobody's ever heard about."

"I've watched a ton of them. They're a lot better than some of the stuff that's on now." His high-pitched voice came clearly through the phone.

Kate moved the receiver again, rolled her eyes, and grinned. "Gotcha, Jake. So your vote makes it unanimous. We're officially calling him Rebel. Thanks—see you later."

"Yep. Absolutely. Affirmative. Right-oh, and all that stuff. I'm trying not to be jealous of all the fun you're having without me."

Kate smiled. "All we've done so far is clean stalls, feed horses, and drink orange juice." She put the phone on speaker so everyone could hear.

"So when are you gonna start trying to solve the case of the missing horses? Leave me a clue or two to follow, will you?"

Colt leaned forward. "No problem, dude. We'll see what we can come up with, then pick your brain when you get here."

"Cool. All right. Adios. See you. Hasta la vista, out of here. Parents are calling. 'Bye." The phone disconnected and a dial tone sounded in Kate's ear.

She laughed. "I always feel like I've walked into a whirlwind when I talk to Jake. I didn't realize it would be the same or worse when we were talking on the phone. Wild."

"Yeah, I hear you," Colt said. "I've been hanging out with him some when I'm not over here. The kid seems kind of lonely, and he and his brother aren't close. From a couple of things Jake has said, I think kids at school treat him like he's a nerd because of his big glasses, the weird stuff he says, and how skinny and small he is. But he's super smart. I can't believe the amount of stuff he's crammed into his head."

"Yeah, I know what you mean," Kate said. "So, what's next?" She turned to her mother. "Did you get any names or information about the other horse owners who've lost horses? I'm trying to figure out how we'll start tracking down clues if we don't know who's lost horses so far."

Her mother shook her head. "Sorry, I didn't, and I'm not sure the sheriff would give me that information. It might be privileged. I'm not sure what you could do to find out."

"Hey, I've got an idea." Tori waved her hand in the air. "Kate, remember the Wilders' barn where we worked for a few weeks before you got your horse and before your mom hired someone to give lessons at your barn?"

Where was her friend headed with her question? "Yeah, but I'm not sure how that helps us."

"Well, the people there are really nice. Maybe we could talk to Mrs. Wilder and see if they lost any horses or know of anyone who did. It would be a place to start."

Melissa's eyes brightened. "Yeah, and we could go to the other two barns in the Odell area, plus maybe check with people we know who own horses. Word spreads in a community like this. If we weren't on summer break, I'm guessing we'd hear about it within a few minutes. In fact," her eyes narrowed, "maybe we should do some snooping with kids our own age or younger. I could see a couple of ten- or eleven-year-old boys thinking this was a fun prank without realizing how much harm they could do. We could start asking around and see what turns up."

Kate shoved her chair back. "Awesome! Mom, is it okay if we ride our horses over to talk to Mrs. Wilder? Maybe we can get ideas of who's been hit. If they're all close by, that would make it easier to figure out. We can go and come right back, or we could stop at a couple of places that Melissa knows about from Pony Club on the way home. We'll take the back roads where there isn't much traffic."

Her mother gave a slight nod. "As long as you aren't gone more than two hours and you ride single file. But what time did Jake think he was going to be able to come over? I'd hate for him to miss you. His house is on the way to Mrs. Wilder's barn, so maybe you can stop by there first. See if he's finished and if his parents will let him go with you. He can always ride his bike ahead of the horses. Tell them you have my permission." She pushed off from the counter. "In fact, I'll give them a call and tell them myself. Jake's a good kid, and he shouldn't get left out of your sleuthing fun, even if it doesn't turn into anything exciting."

Kate's eyes widened. "Nothing exciting? Sheesh, Mom, everything we do is exciting. You never know what's going to happen when the five of us get together to solve a mystery."

Mom's lips drew into a firm line, and she gazed at Kate without saying anything. Kate's heart sank as she saw her mom's wheels turning, probably worrying they were going to get into trouble. She remembered the time they had dumped a bucket of horse manure on her dad's head while trying to catch a thief. And then there was the time Colt almost got buried under a pile of old newspapers at Mr. Wallace's house—and that was only two of their adventures.

"Don't worry, Mom. We promise not to do anything stupid this time, and we'll ask permission before we do anything dangerous—uh—I mean, risky—or stupid—"

Colt poked his elbow in her side. "I think you'd better quit before you dig yourself in any deeper, Kate. Besides, you're starting to sound like Jake. Come on, let's head over to his house and rescue him if we can, then get on the track of the people causing all of the trouble. Who knows how many more horses could be turned loose by tonight if the five of us don't find an answer to what's happening."

CHAPTER FOUR

KATE REINED HER MARE, CAPRI, TO A STOP AT THE end of the sidewalk leading to the two-story house where Jake and his older brother, Jerry, lived with their parents. Memories flooded back as she looked up at Jerry's second-story bedroom window. She shivered, thinking about how close they had come to getting caught while searching Jerry's room for the stolen cash box. They would have been in big trouble if he'd come home a couple of minutes sooner, but thankfully, Jake had been standing guard and covered for them. She'd meant it when she told her mother they wouldn't do anything stupid while they tried to solve this mystery. They'd had enough near misses this summer to last a long time.

Colt pulled up beside her on his quarter horse gelding, Romeo, and swung down. "Want me to go in?"

Kate almost said yes—the last thing she wanted was meet Jerry again. Then she remembered her mom promised to call ahead and talk to Mr. or Mrs. Meyers. "I suppose *I* should, since Mom was going to ask permission for Jake to come with us."

"Right." Colt held Romeo's reins and waited for Melissa and Tori's horses to come up behind him. "We'll wait here, but you'd better tell Jake to put a rush on it. We only have two hours, and we want to stop at as many places as we can."

Tori leaned over Starlight's saddle to grab Kate's reins. "I've got her, Kate. I'm glad Capri and Starlight are pasture buddies. Otherwise, I think I'd get off to hold her."

"Yeah. I know some horses can get pretty nasty to each other when they stand too close. Thanks." Kate walked slowly toward the front door. Right as she raised her hand to press the doorbell, the door flew open and Jake blasted out, nearly knocking her over.

"Wow! Pardon, forgive, sorry, excuse me." Jake's words tumbled over one another as he scrambled to keep his feet, but he didn't quite make it. He vaulted down the last step and landed in a roll on the grass, ending up stretched out, face first, his glasses flying off to the side.

Kate sprang into action and reached Jake at the same time Colt did. She picked up Jake's glasses, which thankfully ᵊren't broken, and Colt picked up Jake. Kate glanced over ᵗshoulder, wondering if Colt had left Romeo on his own.

Not that it would matter, since the horse was trained to stand still if Colt ever dropped his reins. But Melissa stood between Romeo and Mocha, allowing both geldings to graze along the edge of the fence.

Jake dusted himself off, then he pushed his glasses back onto his nose, scrunching his forehead and frowning. "Wow! That was some tumble. When I was a little kid, I used to watch *Thomas the Train*. I mean, a really *little* kid. But there's this one episode where the train goes off the tracks and tumbles over into a field." He grinned at Kate. "Guess you're glad I'm not a train, huh?"

She laughed out loud. "Right, Jake—very glad. If you're okay, we need to get going."

"Sure. I'm perfect. Where are we going, anyway? And I hope you don't expect me to ride a horse!"

"We're going to Mrs. Wilder's barn to ask if she's lost any horses or knows anyone who has," Colt said. "Then we'll stop to see a few people Melissa knows who are Pony Club members. We're hoping to find clues at any places where horses have disappeared. The sheriff's department is stretched pretty thin, and there's no way they're going to be able to stake out a pasture or check every single crime scene for clues. And you can ride your bike in front of the horses, they don't get spooked with you following us."

Jake headed for his bike, which was leaned against the garage. "So we're going on a stakeout? Cool! I've seen them do that in detective shows. I've always wanted to sit and eat donuts and watch for a crime to happen."

Tori giggled. "No donuts this trip, Jake. But hopefully we can stop another crime from happening—who knows?"

Forty-five minutes later, Kate and her friends exited the second barn in Odell that boarded horses or offered lessons. Kate kicked at a rock in the parking area. "I thought we'd find out something. Neither of these barns lost any horses, and nobody seems to know anything."

Tori shook her head, her ponytail swinging with the motion. "Nuh-uh. Remember, Mrs. Wilder said she thinks she knows one person who might have lost a horse, and she told us where they live. Why not go there next?"

Melissa's face brightened. "Yeah. Don't give up yet. They might know something, or maybe they'll let us look around their place and see if we can find any clues."

Kate shrugged. "I suppose. It's only that Mrs. Wilder didn't sound very sure. I hate bothering people, but I guess it isn't going to hurt to knock on their door and ask."

Colt stepped into the stirrup and swung his leg over his saddle. "Right. It's only a little way up the road. Let's go." He took off on Romeo at a trot. "You guys are so slow!" he called over his shoulder.

Determination to catch the trouble-makers surged through Kate. How silly to get discouraged because they didn't find out anything at the first two stops. She urged her mare into a trot and grinned at Tori, who rode beside her. "I'm so thankful for you guys!" She raised her voice as the breeze whipped around her ears. "And I thought when I moved to this area, I wouldn't have any friends."

Tori laughed. "I hear you. I didn't have any close friends till you showed up, and now I have four. Pretty cool! But we'd better spread out. If a car comes we don't want to be in the road."

Jake rode ahead on his bike, with Colt right behind and Melissa brought up the rear. Once they rounded the final corner, they slowed at the end of a short driveway flanked on either side by pasture. Kate saw three horses in the field to the left—a gray, a sorrel, and a black Appaloosa with a spotted blanket across his hip. She pulled Capri to a stop. "This must be the place. The sheriff said a gray was set loose, and I think that's what Mrs. Wilder said, too. What's the name of this person, Colt?"

He looked over his shoulder. "Jackie Dietz. She and her husband show their driving horses sometimes."

Jake panted as he rolled to a stop. "You guys had a hard time keeping up with my high speed on my bike, huh?"

Melissa shook her head and took a motherly tone. "You did great. I was afraid it might be hard for you, since you don't spend a lot of time on your bike."

"Yeah, but since I started hanging out with you guys, I'm getting a lot more exercise." Jake took a swig from the water bottle he'd brought along. "Anyway, what do you mean, driving? She pulls her car with her horses or something?"

Melissa slapped herself on the forehead and laughed. "I forgot you're not a horse person, Jake. The horse pulls a cart or a buggy. They have classes at horse shows for that. Haven't you ever seen one going down the road?"

Jake twisted his lips to the side. "I watched a movie about Amish people once, and I saw a horse pulling a buggy. But nah, I've never seen one in person."

Colt laughed. "Maybe we can get you a ride in one someday. But right now, we need to talk to these people."

"Right. Gotcha. Okie-dokie, no problemo. Let's roll!" Jake jumped on his bike and sprinted down the driveway toward the house, his laugh rolling out behind him.

A couple of minutes later, the group waited at the end of the short driveway holding the horses while Kate and Colt stood in front of the door. Kate drew in her breath, hoping someone would be home and could give them the answers they needed.

The door swung open, and a young woman with red hair pulled into a ponytail gazed at them. "May I help you? Are you doing some kind of fund-raising drive for your school?"

Kate shook her head. "No, ma'am." She decided to get right to the point. "Are you Jackie Dietz?"

"Yes, I am. What's this about?"

"My parents own Blue Ribbon Barn, where we board horses and give lessons, and we had a horse show up at our place. No one has claimed him yet, and we're hoping to find the owner or figure out who's turning horses loose. We stopped at the Wilders' barn, and Mrs. Wilder said your gray Arab mare was returned after being gone for a few hours."

The woman nodded. "That's right. Abby about gave us a heart attack when she disappeared. She's our best driving mare and a state champion. We were so thankful she didn't get stolen and one of the neighbors caught her." She rested h hand on the doorframe. "So you haven't found the owner yet for one that showed up at your barn? What's it look like? I might be able to help."

"It's a gelding. He's a black bay with three black stockings and one white stocking up to his knee. He also has a narrow white blaze down his face, and he's kind of wild. We had a hard time catching him, even though he was wearing a halter. Mom thinks he's fairly young, but she can't be sure. She said she could tell his knees had finished developing, so he's at least three, and maybe older. And he could be a Morgan or a Thoroughbred cross with a Morgan—we're not sure of that, either."

"So no one has reported him to the sheriff as missing? That's strange. I thought they'd returned all the horses by now."

Colt reached down to pluck a long blade of grass growing by the step and fiddled with it. "Nope. Not all of them. Rebel is still at Kate's place."

"Rebel?" The woman's brows rose. "I thought you didn't know anything about the horse."

Colt grinned. "We don't. But that's what we're calling him. So did the sheriff or a deputy come out and look around?"

She shrugged. "A deputy took a report and glanced at the gate that was left open, but that's about it. I don't suppose there's much more they can do. It's not like they can get fingerprints, and even if they did, it's probably a couple of kids out to make mischief—I doubt their prints would be in the system."

"Right," Colt said. "We'd appreciate it if you'd keep an ear open for anyone still missing a horse and send them to Kate's barn. Also, would you mind if we check the ground around your gate and along your fence line for possible clues?"

"Sure, I don't see that it can hurt." She gave a little laugh. "Are you trying to crack the mystery?"

Kate grinned. "Yep. We've solved a couple of other ones this summer, so you never know. We promise we won't open the gate or mess with your horses."

"I wasn't too worried about it. You look like good kids. Besides, I can see the gate from my front window." She pointed in that direction. "Too bad I was still in bed when the gate was opened and Abby got out. I'm so thankful the other two horses were in the other pasture then. Whoever did it must have gotten spooked and didn't have time to open the second gate. We have a hitching rail on the side of the house, if you'd like to tie your horses up before you go look."

Colt lifted his hand in salute. "Thanks. We'll take a look at the area around both gates. You never know—they could have dropped something if they were in a hurry to get away."

CHAPTER FIVE

KATE AND TORI TOOK ONE GATE while Melissa and Jake took the other, and Colt walked along the fence line. Kate knelt next to the wood post, peering at the ground.

Tori leaned over her. "What are you hoping to find?"

Kate shrugged. "I'm not sure. Like Colt said, you never know—someone could have lost a button or an earring or anything."

"Yeah, but even if they did, how does that help us? We can't go to every house in Odell and ask if someone lost their earring."

The air whooshed out of Kate's lungs. "You're right. So this is kinda stupid then, and we're wasting our time."

Tori plopped down beside her on the grass. "No way is it stupid, although I'm not sure what we'd do with a clue like that. But we might find something else."

"Hey, guys!" Colt waved his hand. "I found a picture."

"Of what?" Kate scrambled to her feet, her heart racing.

"It's a dog and a little kid."

The rest of the group gathered around Colt as he sat on the ground, straining to see the photo he was holding. Jake leaned over Colt's shoulder and adjusted his glasses. "Do you recognize the kid? Maybe that'll tell us who was here."

"Nope, never seen him before." Colt held the picture up so they could see it better.

Kate stared at the wallet-sized photo. "Looks like it's seen better days—it's kinda wrinkled and beat up. We should probably ask Mrs. Dietz if it's hers. Besides, how would someone lose a picture when they were unlatching a gate?"

Melissa bent over to look more closely. "I've seen a dog like that somewhere, but then again, lots of golden retrievers look alike." She put her hands in her pockets. "They could have pulled wire cutters out of their pocket like this, or removed something else, and the photo fell out too."

"I've lost a ton of things, including money, when I put stuff in a pocket with something else and forgot it was there. It's easy to do." Tori's eyes scanned the ground around her.

Kate headed toward the house. "Let's check with Mrs. Dietz. If it's not hers, maybe we have our first clue."

Jackie Dietz answered almost before Kate could press the doorbell. "Did you find anything?" She looked slightly amused, as though she didn't expect a positive response.

Colt stepped forward. "Yes. Did you lose this picture? Or do you know who this is?"

Her smile faded, and she leaned over to look. "No. It isn't mine, and I've never seen that boy before. You think maybe the people who did this lost it?"

"It's possible," Colt said. "Sure wish we could find something else."

Mrs. Dietz pursed her lips and leaned against the door frame. "I might be able to help. I called a friend who also lost a horse. Her name is Carol Mason. She lives up the road about a quarter mile—three driveways down from our place, across the road. She said it's fine if you come check out the area around their fence and gate. Her gate was locked, but her fence was actually cut. She knows you're coming so you don't have to stop at her house, since it's a ways up the drive. I told her five kids on horses and a bike would stop by in a few minutes. Sound okay?"

"That's great," Melissa said. "Thank you for all your help."

"Yes, thanks." Kate echoed her words and headed toward Capri, suddenly anxious to get going now that they had their first clue. If only they could find the person in the photo, they might be able to solve this crime.

An hour later, Kate and her friends rode into the parking area in front of her family's barn, discouraged that they hadn't found any new clues at their last stop. Kate wasn't too surprised to see three cars parked at the barn, since boarders were always coming and going.

Her mom hurried out to meet them. "Kate, we have two new boarders who are doing their paperwork now, and a couple of people are here taking lessons. One of the trainers wants to use the round pen where we put Rebel instead of the big arena, since it's busy right now. She has a new student and doesn't want him spooked by too much activity. Somehow we need to move Rebel, but I don't want anyone getting hurt. I wish his owner had turned up and claimed him."

Kate crossed her arms. "There's no way we can move Rebel. Honestly, Mom, the trainer needs to use the indoor arena or the big outdoor one. Besides, if we move him to a stall, he might go nuts in there."

"You're right. I wasn't thinking. As soon as you put your horse away, can you make sure the two empty stalls at the far end of the barn have shavings in them? And maybe put fresh hay in, since the new people will be bringing their horses in the next hour or so. Thanks, kids. We'll talk about your day later. I need to get back inside."

"Wow, your mom was stressed." Tori shook her head. "That's not normal for her. I can't believe she even considered trying to move Rebel."

"Yeah," Kate said, "she's been a little freaked out ever since Pete left for camp. I think she misses him a lot and is worried about how he's doing. I'm sure glad he'll only be gone a couple more days. It's not the same without him around. Hey, if you guys need to head home, I understand. I'd better check on those stalls."

Jake still straddled his bike. "I need to get home. Mom wanted more help with the yard and only cut me loose for an hour or two."

Melissa nodded. "Yep, me too. Do we have anything else we can check out? And what are we going to do about Rebel? It's weird to leave him in the round pen all the time and never brush him or anything."

Colt swung his leg over his saddle and stepped to the ground. "I can stay and help you, Kate. And maybe we can come up with an idea or two about finding Rebel's owner."

Tori dismounted and moved her horse toward the barn. "Me too. Mom didn't care if I stayed most of the day. Besides, I'd like to stand outside the fence next to Rebel and see if he'll take carrots from my hand. Maybe we can start taming him so we can catch him easier next time."

Kate felt a stirring of hope at the idea. "Okay. I appreciate the help, Colt. And Tori, the carrots are in the drawer in the fridge, if you want to grab a couple after we unsaddle. I'm not sure what our next step is. Maybe sleep on it and see what we can come up with in the next day or two. I can't believe I'm about to say this, but it feels like we've run out of ideas."

CHAPTER SIX

TWO DAYS LATER, KATE AND TORI stood in the driveway, waiting for Kate's mom to return with Pete. Kate bounced on her toes, so eager she could barely stand it. She had missed Pete so much.

She looped her hand through Tori's arm, wishing again that she'd chosen to go with her mom. "It's too bad everyone else couldn't be here to see Pete, but I'm kind of glad we'll have him to ourselves at first." She reached down to pat Rufus, their German shepherd. "You're glad he's almost home too, huh boy?"

The dog gave a soft yip, and his tail whipped back and forth.

Tori turned wide chocolate eyes on Kate. "Would you rather I go home? I never thought about you wanting to spend time with Pete alone."

Kate shook her head hard. "No way! I'm glad your mom didn't care if I spent the last couple of hours at your house, and even happier she let you come back with me. It's more fun sharing good stuff with a friend."

Tori bumped Kate's shoulder with hers. "Yep. No kidding. Hey, here comes your car!"

They both rushed forward with Rufus on their heels, stopping next to the round pen where Rebel trotted in circles, tossing his head and snorting.

The car slid to a smooth stop nearby, and Kate hurried to the back passenger door closest to her. She could see Pete looking out, but no excited expression broke the solemn planes of his face. She'd hoped with all her heart that camp would make a change in Pete's behavior, but he had the same blank look he'd worn before leaving. Hadn't anything changed at all this past week? Had the entire experience been a waste of money?

Kate's heart cried out to God once again, shooting up a little prayer for her brother. This was so hard. Why did Pete have to be this way? Why couldn't he be a normal, pesky little brother who got into her stuff, pulled her braid, made messes he refused to clean up, and talked too much? What she wouldn't give to have those kind of problems.

She drew in a deep breath and whispered. "Thank you, Lord, for my little brother, just the way he is. No matter what, I love him."

Tori moved up beside her. "Did you say something, Kate?"

"A quick prayer for Pete," Kate replied.

"Good idea," Tori said. "We need to do that more, huh? God is able to help him. Maybe we should focus on that, instead of what a camp could do for him."

Amazement hit Kate. Tori seemed to understand what she was feeling more than anyone she knew. It was beyond awesome having a friend who was also a Christian and who shared her faith in God as well as her love for her little brother.

"Thanks, I needed to hear that. And you're right—maybe we can all start praying."

Slowly, so she wouldn't startle Pete, she pulled up on the car door's latch at the same time her mother exited the driver's seat. Since her dad had to work today, Mom had gone alone. Kate had asked to go along and see the camp, but Mom didn't want to overwhelm Pete. That was another good reason only Tori was here, and not all four of her friends.

"Hey there, buddy," Kate said in a low, calm voice. "How're you doing? Glad to be home?"

Pete gave a slow nod and climbed out of the car, but he didn't stop beside her as she'd expected. Instead he walked straight to the corral where Rebel still snorted and pawed at the ground. "A new horse."

Kate walked slowly to his side and knelt next to him. "Yes. His name is Rebel. But he's very scared of people."

Her mom came to sit cross-legged on Pete's other side. "Pete, Rebel is not tame. He's very wild, and we must stay away from him. You can't go in with Rebel, not ever. Do you understand?"

Pete nodded, but he didn't take his gaze off the horse. "He likes Pete. Pete likes Rebel."

Kate's heart lurched. That was the same kind of thing he'd said about Jake's huge Saint Bernard not long ago when he'd first met the half-grown puppy. The family had worried that Mouse and their own dog, Rufus, would get in a fight, and that Pete might be caught in the middle since he was out in the yard playing when Mouse arrived. But somehow Mouse and Rufus had formed a friendship, and Kate was still convinced it was her little brother who had brought it about. He seemed to sense things about certain animals while completely ignoring other ones.

"Rebel would probably like you if he was tame, Pete. But Mom is right. He's wild, and he's not safe." She touched his arm, hoping he'd respond to her touch, but he didn't move. "So don't try to pet him or anything, okay?"

He didn't reply. Her mom glanced across his head at Kate. "We'll need to keep a close eye on him—and on the horse. He's a pretty determined boy."

Tori grinned. "Yeah—remember how he was when you wanted your own horse, Kate? He decided he was going to make it happen and worried all of us sick."

"Exactly." Kate's mom stood up. "Come on, Pete. Let's take your bag into the house and get unpacked, and then you can have a snack. I think I even have a bag of M&M's that Melissa left for you, since she couldn't be here today."

Pete didn't budge, not even at the mention of his favorite candy. Kate couldn't believe it. M&M's would lure him away from almost anything.

The little boy edged closer to the fence. "Rebel is my friend. Rufus is my friend." He reached out to Rufus and patted his head. "Mouse is my friend. Rebel likes me."

Kate gaped at her mother. "Mom," she whispered, "did you hear that?"

Her mother nodded, her eyes wide.

Tori eased closer. "What did I miss? What happened?"

Kate turned to her, hope once more pounding through her veins. "Pete didn't say Rufus is Pete's friend, or Rebel likes

Pete like he always does. He said me—*me*, Tori! Maybe something good came from that camp after all." She squatted next to Pete again. "Yes, little guy. You have a lot of friends. How about you go in the house with Mom, and Tori and I will give your new friend some hay. You can come out later, and if Mom says it's okay, we can try to give Rebel a carrot on your hand. Horses like carrots." She raised a brow at her mother, who nodded. "But you have to promise never, ever to try to do anything alone with Rebel. Okay, buddy?"

Pete didn't answer, but he kept his hand on Rufus's head. The dog's face was split in a huge doggy smile, though Pete remained solemn. "Rebel is my friend."

Kate lolled on a lawn chair under their big shade tree a couple of days later with her four friends gathered around, sitting and lying on the grass and other chairs. The temperatures had soared into the low nineties, and none of them felt like moving. At least it was late afternoon, and hopefully, at their higher elevation, the temperature would start cooling soon.

She fanned herself with her hand, but it didn't produce any relief. "This heat is a killer."

The silence that greeted her words made her sit up and look around. "What? Did you all fall asleep?"

Colt rolled over on his stomach, then stuck a piece of grass in the corner of his mouth. "Hmm. Pretty sweet. I see why horses like this stuff. Definitely better than straw."

"Yuk!" Melissa slugged his shoulder. "Why don't you chew gum or something?" She didn't wait for him to answer, but turned to Kate. "So Pete's been home a couple of days now. How's he doing? Have you seen any change? Maybe we can get him to come out in the yard and sit in your little pool or something. I didn't realize how much I'd miss that kid until he was gone."

"That makes two of us. We've seen a couple of changes in the way he talks—the biggest is he's started saying me instead of calling himself Pete. That's pretty huge, at least to us. But the weird thing is, he seems to be fixated on Rebel, the same way he was with Mouse when he first met him."

The big dog lay sprawled next to Jake. When he heard his name, he raised his head, his eyes bleary and barely focusing on Kate, then he lowered it again and closed his eyes.

Kate chuckled and reached over to pet him. "Poor Mouse. He has an even thicker coat than Rufus does. He must be miserable in this heat."

Melissa sat up and stretched her arms out wide, as if she could catch a breeze. "So any more clues or any phone calls about Rebel? What does the sheriff think?"

Jake scooted over to a tree and leaned against it. "Yeah, I've been meaning to ask you that, since it's been a few days since we did any—what did you call it—sleuthing? I think I heard that in an old mystery movie once. Searching. Hunting for clues. Snooping. Spying. Right?"

"Yep," Kate said with a chuckle. "It's a weird word, but it fits, Jake. By the way, guys, Dad called the sheriff again, and get this—"

All four heads turned her way, and even Mouse opened his eyes again, but Rufus snored and didn't move.

"The sheriff told Dad this morning that all the horses had been returned to their homes, and nothing else had happened. Until last night. A stall door was opened last night, along with another pasture gate opened and one fence cut. Two of the horses still haven't been reported as found. Is that crazy, or what? I mean, we all assumed it was over."

"So now what?" Tori broke her silence, her brown eyes wide. "Do we start hunting again?"

"I'm all for it, if you guys are. Dad actually got a name of both the owners whose horses are still missing, so if one of the horses shows up here, we can call the owner. Mom said it's weird that all of them are within a mile or so of each other." Kate planted her hands on her hips. "That makes me think that Rebel's owner must live nearby, so why haven't they come forward?"

Colt grunted. "Maybe the horse is too much work, and they don't want him anymore."

Jake shook his head. "Naw, horses are expensive. They could always sell Rebel if they didn't want him. No one's gonna throw away a horse. That's crazy. Although I did see this show once—"

"Jake!" Kate, Tori, Melissa, and Colt all shouted the word at the same time—and then they burst out laughing.

Kate finally got control of herself and gave Jake a warm smile. "We love the way you know everything about movies and TV, but maybe we need to think about solving *this* mystery. Right?"

His face beamed. "You guys love my knowledge, huh? Cool! I'm sure I can come up with a ton more examples about all sorts of stuff. Just last night I was thinking—"

"Jake!" The chorus rang out again, and this time Jake joined in the laugh.

"Right. Got it. Understood. Agreed. Let it go." He gave a deep sigh. "But it's so hard not to share."

Colt poked him with his elbow. "We think you're brilliant and all that, but it's time to get to work on the problem at hand. Let's see if we can find another clue."

CHAPTER SEVEN

THE NEXT DAY, KATE AND HER friends scouted the area where the fence had been cut, looking for any sign of who had been there. Kate put her hands on her hips. "Do you think the sheriff has already been out here? I see a gum wrapper, but it could belong to anyone."

Colt started walking along the fence line, and then he called back over his shoulder. "Remember the picture we found? It wasn't by the gate. I think we need to scout the whole area. What if they planned to cut the fence somewhere else, then got spooked? You never know what we might find if they took off in a hurry."

Melissa pointed at the hot wire fence. "How do you suppose they cut this without getting shocked? You can see where it's been patched here."

Jake came up beside her. "That's easy—a pair of loppers with rubber handles like my dad uses for yard work. They would snip that wire in a heartbeat, and you'd never get shocked."

"Right," Melissa agreed. "But why? I mean, I don't get it. If it *is* a bunch of kids, and I'm leaning toward older teens, what do they have to gain? Wouldn't all of this lose its thrill after the first night? You know, kind of like egging mailboxes or stuff? The first night it might be fun, but after that, it's lame."

Tori walked past, her head bent, examining the ground. She paused and looked up. "Maybe they like the attention it's getting from the sheriff's department. And a story was even in the Hood River News. A lot of kids like attention, even if their names aren't connected with it. Maybe they think they're a bunch of outlaws and a wanted poster will go up soon—who knows?"

Colt moved farther down the fence, kicking at the high grass in the ditch between the fence and the road. "That's a good explanation, Tori. Some kids are ignored by their parents and left alone for hours after school. They might be hoping to get attention, even if it's negative. They also might think it's funny, and they're bragging to a few of their closest friends."

"I don't think it's a bit funny or cool to destroy someone else's property and put their horses in danger," Kate huffed. "And look at Rebel. We still don't know who owns him. We need to go on a door knocking campaign soon and see if we can find anyone who recognizes him or knows the owner. We could take a picture on Mom's cell phone and show it to everyone."

Melissa groaned. "I wish my mom wasn't broke all the time, so I could have my phone back."

"My mom won't allow me to have one until I can pay for it myself," Tori said, rolling her eyes. "My dad works two jobs now trying to make ends meet."

Colt nodded. "Yep. Mine too."

"Don't feel bad, Melissa," Kate chimed in. "My parents said maybe next year. Getting the barn up and running this spring and summer took more money than they expected, and they aren't excited about putting out more for a cell phone for me. But I know Mom won't care if I use hers to show people Rebel's picture."

Jake waved his arms in the air. "Hey, guys! Come look at this. I think I found something."

Kate and her friends raced toward him, where he stood about fifty feet past Colt. Somehow Jake had wandered on down the road without anyone noticing, while they talked about phones and photos.

Kate slid to a stop next to Colt, who had already halted next to Jake. "So what's up? Colt, did you already see whatever Jake found? You think it's anything?"

Colt leaned over and parted the grass, then plucked out something shiny and held it up. "It's a wristband, and it has two initials on it with a dash between. K-M."

Kate and the girls crowded around the two boys. Kate narrowed her eyes and touched the heavy silver band. "It could be either a boy's or a girl's."

"And are the initials for the person who owns it or someone they like?" Melissa winced. "This doesn't get us much farther than we were before. It almost looks like a K plus M, but I think it's a dash."

Jake held out his hand, and Colt gave the band to him. "If my brother Jerry was a few years younger, I'd say he's one of our culprits, and the wristband or bracelet—whatever you want to call it—belonged to his girlfriend. He would've played pranks by letting horses out when he was fourteen or fifteen. But now that he's in college, he's only interested in cars and girls. Besides, he doesn't wear stuff like this."

Kate's hopes, which had risen so high when Jake said he'd found something, plummeted. Were they ever going to figure out who was doing this or who owned Rebel? She shot up a little prayer asking for help, knowing that God was listening.

"That stinks," she sighed. "It would have been nice to have at least one person figured out, since that would likely lead us to the rest. But hey, we're not going to give up yet, right? We need to keep looking."

Tori hadn't spoken a word but was still kicking the grass and inspecting the ground along the length of the fence. "Hey! The grass is all trampled like people were standing here waiting. It's several feet off the road and in a ditch, so there's no way anybody would want to walk down there. And it's only a dozen feet or so from where the fence was cut." She bent over and examined the base of a post and then stood, holding up an empty metallic sports bottle with the logo of a popular team. "I can't see someone tossing this from their car, or the silver band, either."

Melissa walked over to Tori and asked to see the bottle. "This bottle is insulated, not cheap plastic. A lot of kids have these at school, but there's no way someone is going to ditch it. Think this is related to the fence cutting?"

Jake grinned. "Yeah! We might even have the suspect's fingerprints or DNA. But now the cops will have to test you girls and take your prints too, since you're messing with the evidence without gloves on. Don't you ever watch TV?"

Colt shook his head. "Some of us do homework, ride our horses, and hang out with our friends, Jake. You need to ease up on the TV, know what I mean? Besides, now that most of the horses are back home, I can't see the sheriff's department spending the money on DNA tests when they probably think it's a couple of kids playing pranks."

"But we need to keep trying to figure it out," Kate said, "even if they don't care." All of this made her angry. What if Capri had disappeared and they couldn't find her? Or Starlight, Tori's horse, or any of her friends' horses? This kind of stupid prank was unforgiveable. She wanted the kids—or whoever it was—to get caught and punished. They deserved it.

Right then, Kate caught movement from the corner of her eye, and she turned and looked across the road. She shaded her eyes against the glare of the summer sun, wishing she could see better. A movement caught her eye. A man wearing a backpack and walking a golden retriever moved briskly in the opposite direction from them, and he didn't so much as slow when Kate lifted a hand in greeting. Strange—most people in this area were friendlier than that.

She nudged Colt. "Take a look across the road. Did you ever see that guy before?"

Her question caused not only Colt to look, but her other three friends as well. No one spoke a word as the man with the dog moved away from them. Colt shook his head. "Not that I know of. Why?"

Kate shrugged. "I'm not sure. There's something familiar—or strange—about him."

Melissa snickered. "I think it's kind of strange that he's wearing nice loafers, khakis, and a button-up shirt while he's hauling around a loaded backpack and a sleeping bag—and leading a dog. Who walks around in clothes like that if they're out camping?"

"He definitely doesn't look homeless," Jake said, his hands on his hips as he gazed after the man. "Maybe he's one of those guys out to see how far he can walk or something."

Melissa raised her brows. "Wearing loafers? That's got to be killing his feet. Doesn't make sense to me."

"Maybe we should have talked to him." Tori wrinkled her nose. "If he's walking through the area, you never know what he might have noticed."

"I waved at him," Kate said. "But he didn't wave back—he kept on walking like we weren't here."

"Maybe he doesn't talk to strangers," Tori said, giggling. "We're not supposed to."

"I wish I could figure it out." Kate stared down the road. "He's out of sight now, but did something about him or that dog look familiar to you guys?"

Colt and the girls shook their heads, but Jake hesitated. "You still have that picture we found the other day near one of the places a horse was let out?"

Colt poked his hand in his hip pocket and pulled out a slender wallet. He flipped it open. "Yeah. Here you go. What's up?"

Jake scanned it. "I hardly ever forget a face, and when I see a picture, it kind of sticks in my mind." He held it up for their inspection. "Am I crazy, or did that dog he was walking look like the same dog in this picture? I know there are a lot of retrievers in the world, and he's not a little kid, but that could be the twin of this one."

They all looked at the photo, and Kate's stomach knotted. "Yeah, it sure could. What are the odds? A strange guy walks by with a bedroll, a full backpack, and a look-alike dog, strolling right by the scene of one of the crimes."

Jake nearly jumped up and down in his excitement. "Criminals do that all the time. They like to see if anyone is onto them, and they like to gloat over the fact that they got away with something. This could be our guy!"

Colt held up his hand. "Slow down now, detective. He was dressed pretty nice, so he's not some homeless guy going around trying to stir up trouble, or opening gates because he's camping in a pasture and not being careful. He looked the same age as my uncle's age—maybe thirty, if that. Not like some hardened criminal."

The knot slowly started to unravel in the pit of Kate's stomach. "Yeah, you're probably right, and we're jumping to conclusions. Oh well, it was a good idea for a few seconds there. But we can't go chasing down strangers and accusing them of things when we don't have any proof."

Jake narrowed his eyes. "What if that sports bottle was his, and he came back here hoping to find it? Maybe that's why he didn't say hi or wave, because he was hoping we'd leave soon and he could find it. I say we stash it in the grass where we found it—we keep the bracelet but toss the bottle, then hide out in the trees across the road and see if he comes back."

Colt grabbed a handful of grass, yanked it, then chose one blade and put it between his teeth. "Nah, what's that gonna prove? He can walk wherever he wants to. If he finds a water bottle and keeps it, that's no proof it was his in the first place. If he does keep it, then we're out a piece of potential evidence. Sorry, Jake, but I think we're pushing it on this one. We'll keep our eyes open, see if this guy stays in the area, and if we see him again. But I don't think we should assume someone is guilty because they have a dog that looks like the one in the picture."

Jake's shoulders slumped, and he kicked at the grass. "Right. Agreed. Certainly. Guess I was stupid—I'm no detective. Sorry."

Tori's head whipped up, and she tapped Jake on the chest with her finger. "You are *not* stupid, so don't ever say that about yourself. We need to investigate any clues we find, even if they don't lead anywhere. Maybe this one didn't pay off, but that doesn't mean the next one won't. Keep thinking and watching, Jake. You might end up being our star detective yet!"

Thirty minutes later Kate and her friends rode their bikes onto the gravel parking area next to her barn and parked them in the bike rack. She swung to face her friends, the wind blowing her hair. "I promised Pete he could try to feed carrots to Rebel, then I forgot to do it. Want to come with me? If that horse stays around here much longer, we'll need to try to tame him if we can. He needs to be brushed, his mane is getting tangled, and his hooves are a little long."

Colt whistled. "I can't even imagine a horseshoer getting close to that horse with nippers or a hammer. I wonder if he's ever had shoes on. It's not gonna be easy, that's for sure. Look how he acted when you only clipped a lead rope on his halter."

"I know. And it was kinda dumb of me to go in with a strange horse I knew nothing about."

Colt gave her a quick tap on the shoulder with his fist. "But you'll know better next time, and that's good, right?"

She grinned. "Right. Thanks for not making me feel worse. Stay here a sec, you guys—I'll get Pete."

She dashed to the house, praying her little brother would be in the mood to come. The kids loved Pete, and she knew how much they wanted to help make him happy. Stopping in the kitchen first, she took two long carrots out of a bag in the fridge and then went in search of Pete.

A couple of minutes later, she exited the house with the little guy by her side. He was as excited as she'd seen him in a long time about anything. "*I* will feed Rebel the carrots." His gaze didn't quite meet hers but skittered on past.

Kate still felt a thrill at his use of me instead of Pete. The family had noticed less humming and frustration in Pete since he'd returned from camp as well, so some of what he'd experienced there must be helping. Mom and Dad were supposed to meet with one of the camp counselors this weekend to talk about continuing some of the games and therapy they'd started, so he wouldn't lose ground. Kate was willing to help with anything she could. Pete was such a special little brother, and she wanted him to be able to experience life as fully as possible, in every way he could, as he grew up.

They neared the fence where Rebel nosed hay in a corner nearest them. Melissa stepped forward. "Hey, Pete. I brought M&M's for you today. Want some?"

Pete shook his head and kept moving toward the corral bars, his gaze fastened on Rebel. "No M&M's. Carrots for Rebel. Rebel is my friend."

Colt turned wide eyes on Kate. "He said 'my friend,' not 'Pete's friend.' And three complete sentences—well, almost complete. You know what I mean. Wow! I'm not sure I've ever heard him talk this much."

Kate smiled. "Not often, that's for sure. There's something special about Rebel, Mouse, and Rufus that seem to change Pete. I wish we could discover what it is and make magic dust out of it and sprinkle it on him all the time."

Jake's head bobbed up and down. "Yeah, like Tinker Bell in *Peter Pan*. Wouldn't it be cool to be one of the lost boys and live on an island and never grow old and play all the time and—"

Colt elbowed him playfully. "Hey, dude, take a breath. That's one long sentence. We aren't little kids anymore, you know." He grinned. "But chasing pirates and swimming in a lagoon and fishing all the time would be cool."

Pete ignored them all, darting toward the fence and sticking his arm through the bars, hand out flat. "Rebel." He whispered the word, but Kate still heard him. "Come see me. Pete is your friend."

Kate's heart sank. He shouldn't be that close, but she didn't want to pull him back and possibly scare him. And why had he said 'Pete is your friend' instead of 'I am your friend'? Was it too much to hope that he was improving? Had God heard her prayers for her little brother? Did He care?

She looked around at her friends and felt a little surge of joy. Of course God cared. He'd brought this awesome group of friends into her life, and He'd already answered many of her prayers. Maybe Pete was exactly the way he was supposed to be for some reason she didn't understand. After all, just because she didn't get a yes, that didn't mean God wasn't listening or answering. At least, that's what her dad always told her.

She moved slowly toward Pete, keeping her voice low. "Hey, buddy, how about you pull your hand back in? I'll give you a carrot you can feed to Rebel, but you don't want to stick your hand in there with him. We don't know if he might bite you." She saw him stiffen and hurried to explain. "Not that he'd do it on purpose to hurt you, but even nice horses can make a mistake."

Pete didn't move but kept his arm extended into the corral. He started to croon an almost sing-songy refrain to the big gelding. "Rebel is my friend. Come see me, Rebel. You are my friend. Come, Rebel. You are my friend."

Kate was almost to Pete when the big bay raised his head from the nearby pile of hay and gave a low nicker. He moved forward with a slow grace, his neck stretched toward the little boy, his nostrils flaring. Kate gasped, ready to lunge at her brother and jerk him away, even if it scared him. "Pete. Move away now. Come here with me."

Pete appeared to have pulled completely into his own world. "Come, Rebel."

The horse dropped his head low and shoved it against Pete's hand, and Kate almost thought she heard a sigh escape his lips.

Pete stroked Rebel's face and rubbed under his forelock, then ran his hand all the way down to the horse's nose and lips. Kate stiffened. Would the gelding snap his head up and race away? She moved close and put her hand on Pete's shoulder. "Pete, we need to move back. This horse is wild. He doesn't want to be petted."

But somehow Rebel seemed to have changed. Kate saw it happen as soon as Pete's voice reached his ears. He pressed his face harder into her brother's palm and dropped his head lower still, allowing Pete to fondle his ears while crooning that sing-song refrain.

Melissa, Colt, Jake, and Tori all moved to the fence. Tori stopped right next to Kate and leaned close. "I can't believe what I'm seeing. Where did the wild horse go? Did someone take him in the night and bring another one?"

Jake pushed his glasses up on his nose. "Have you guys seen that *Dog Whisperer* show? Maybe Pete is a horse whisperer. I've heard there really is such a thing. It's like they understand each other. Really weird, but kinda cool, right?"

The door slammed on the house, and Kate's mom appeared on the step, shading her eyes. "Are you guys finished feeding Rebel carrots? Pete needs to come in and take a bath." She walked forward and then froze. "What in the world? Kate, get Pete away from that wild animal before it takes his hand off!"

CHAPTER EIGHT

KATE LEANED AGAINST THE ARENA FENCE in the morning sun, watching Rebel. She couldn't believe the horse had been here almost ten days now and no one had come forward to claim him. The rest of the family still couldn't get near him, not even to pet him, but he would run to the fence nickering whenever Pete came out of the house and called his name.

She shook her head, then reached down to stroke Rufus's head, fondling the big dog's ears. "Like Jake said, it's kinda weird."

"What's weird?" Tori spoke from behind her.

Kate grabbed her chest. "Wow! You scared me. When did you get here? I can't believe I didn't see you ride up."

"I didn't ride. My mom dropped me off at the house. She's going grocery shopping, and I told her I'd rather hang out with you. Your mom said it's okay, so here I am. Besides, we still haven't solved either of the mysteries, and it's bothering me."

"That makes two of us."

"Hey, guys!" Colt's voice caused both girls to turn his direction. "I called your mom and told her I was bored. Then I called Jake after your mom said it was fine to come over. He's on his way. Anyone hear from Melissa?"

Kate laughed, loving that her friends felt comfortable enough to hang out here when they were bored. She never had friends like this in Spokane, and she never knew what she was missing. And to think she'd been so upset at having to move to a new area. Now she felt thankful for what God had done in her life. It hadn't made a bit of sense at the time, but wasn't that exactly what seemed to happen so often? She'd heard her mom say that to her dad more than once — "What we thought was going to be bad, God turned to something good." Now was that awesome, or what? She couldn't help grinning.

Jake screeched to a halt on his bike, sending fine gravel flying and the girls screaming and running. "Oops. Sorry. I wanted to make an entrance, not cause you guys to make an exit." He pushed his glasses up and peered around. "Where's Melissa?"

"That's what Colt asked—if anyone has heard from Melissa," Kate said. "I didn't know any of you guys were going to show up. Tori surprised me first, then Colt, so I didn't know to call her. But we probably should. We need to do more work on our mysteries, and I don't want to leave her out."

"Want me to run in the house and ask to use your phone? I can call her real quick," Tori said

"Sure! We promise not to talk about anything important till you get back." Kate mimed pulling a zipper across her tightly closed lips.

"Right." Tori drew out the word. "I can see the three of you keeping quiet the whole time I'm gone."

Colt raised two fingers pressed together. "Scout's honor. But only for two minutes, so you'd better run."

Tori ran. She returned in just over the two minutes allowed, panting for breath. "Melissa's coming. Her mom is going shopping, and Melissa didn't want to go, so she's having her mom drop her off. Sounds like this is the day for shopping trips. I'm glad I didn't get dragged along on one."

"Ugh. Me too," Kate said, rolling her eyes. "Not that I don't like new clothes and stuff, but I'd rather be outside with my friends than stuck in a store or the car."

A few minutes later, Melissa's mom dropped her off. Kate pulled her mom's phone out of her pocket and waved it in the air. "Let's get a couple of shots of Rebel and see if we can find his owner. Maybe the person is on a long vacation and whoever is taking care of him isn't paying attention or checking to see if he's still there."

"Yeah, like with Capri, Kate. The lady had died, and her husband didn't know anything about horses. It's a good thing we found her, or she might have starved." Tori moved into step beside Kate on the way to the small corral.

"Yeah, or ended up sold at an auction and maybe going for dog food." Kate shuddered, still hating the thought of what her wonderful horse had gone through. "Capri is one of the biggest answers to prayer I've ever had."

Melissa nudged Kate's arm. "What's that supposed to mean? You were praying for Capri before you guys saved her? I don't get it."

"No," Kate said, "but I'd been asking God for a horse of my own for a long time. Mom and Dad said they couldn't afford to buy one, and while we were living in Spokane, we would have had to pay to board one, and that was super expensive. At first I was upset that we moved here—until I saw the big barn and all the pasture, but Mom and Dad still said no. They spent a lot of money moving and had other expenses. I almost gave up, but Pete wanted me to have a horse of my own, too. It was partly because of him that I kept praying and asking for an answer." She smiled. "Then God showed Capri to Tori and me, and then Mr. Miller decided to give her to me after she escaped and showed up here. Pretty amazing, huh?"

Melissa nodded. "No kidding. Like something out of a book. Until I met you guys, I didn't even know God or prayer was real."

Colt stepped to the other side of Melissa. "Yep. We all have good stories to tell about answers to prayer, but right now, we probably better take those pictures and head out. Who knows—we might be the answer to someone else's prayer when we return the horse they love and don't even know is missing."

Kate was getting tired of knocking on doors and getting the same answer. Not a single person had seen Rebel before or knew who might own him. They couldn't keep a horse that belonged to somebody else, but what else were they supposed to do? Maybe it was time to pray again. She sighed. Why was it that she always thought about prayer as the last resort? Hopefully she'd think of it sooner next time.

The group of friends stood in front of another house after getting another "No, sorry," from the homeowner. Colt picked up his bike off the lawn, his usually happy expression twisted into resignation. "I wonder if we're going about this the wrong way."

Tori scrunched her forehead. "What's that mean? How else can we show Rebel's picture and find out who owns him?"

"I don't know." Colt took off his hat and ran his hand through his hair. "Maybe run the photo in the newspaper under 'horse found' or something? And we haven't shown the pictures to the barns in the area. I think they'd know more about the missing horses than anyone."

Jake adjusted his glasses. "Colt has a good point. I'm not a horse person, so I never notice a horse in a pasture."

Melissa groaned. "And you have no idea what you're missing either, Jake. Life doesn't get much better than when you're on horseback."

"Especially if you're in a Western saddle hitting the trails." Colt grinned at Melissa.

She gave him a mock scowl. "No. An English saddle riding over jumps. That's the best!"

"Whatever," Tori said with a giggle. "I think Jake and Colt are both right. Before Kate got me interested in horses, I didn't look at them much either, except sometimes I'd notice how pretty one looked running across a field. So maybe we are going about this wrong."

Kate eyed her. "So we go back to the barns and show the picture? Okay, I guess that makes more sense than what we're doing now. Let's go."

CHAPTER NINE

KATE AND HER FRIENDS LEFT THE last barn, disappointed that Mrs. Wilder wasn't there and they'd have to return the following day. Rebel wasn't getting any tamer hanging out in their corral, and she couldn't even imagine how they'd move him to his owner's house. Of course, whoever owned him probably didn't have any trouble with him at all. Who knows, his real name might be Angel. She couldn't help but chuckle at the thought.

Tori looked up from swinging her leg over her bike. "What's so funny? I thought you were disappointed we didn't find Rebel's owner yet."

"Yeah, I am." Kate sobered at her friend's reminder. "I was thinking his real name might be something like Angel instead of Rebel. Weird, huh?"

Jake hopped on his bike. "Nope. Not weird at all. There have been a bunch of strange names for horses in movies—in fact, for a lot of different animals. I can give you a list if you'd like."

"Nope." Kate looked over her shoulder, checking for traffic on the rural road. "But thanks anyway. Right now I'm trying to figure out what we do next."

She stood on one pedal and shoved off, her friends following. They traveled down the road a short distance and rounded a corner. Kate slowed when she saw two figures just ahead. The man they'd seen not long ago with the backpack and the dog were coming toward them—on their side of the road. Would he duck into the brush and take off? If he was guilty of letting the horses out, he probably would. Then again, maybe he'd play it cool and not want anyone to suspect him. Her heart rate increased. Maybe that was why he was wearing nice clothes. He was only pretending to be a tourist passing through.

She slowed to a stop on the shoulder and waited for him to approach. Tires skidding on the loose gravel sounded behind her as Colt drew to a stop next to her. He leaned toward her and whispered, "What's up? You wanna talk to this guy?"

She shrugged, not sure what she was planning. Maybe she didn't have a plan, but talking couldn't hurt, could it? After all, there was safety in numbers, and the dog didn't look vicious. In fact, his tail was wagging, and his mouth hung open in a big doggy grin. As the man drew close, she waved. She could feel her friends gathered beside and behind her.

"Hi." She couldn't think of another thing to say.

The man halted, and his dog gave a soft woof. "Hi. Nice day for a bike ride. I should get me one of those instead of walking everywhere." He cocked his head to the side. He didn't look scary or like a criminal—in fact, he looked pretty normal, with warm eyes.

Kate's first thought was to grip her handlebars tighter as a bit of nervousness set in. How silly. She'd been told not to talk to strangers, but what could he do? Grab her bike and ride off down the road with everyone watching? "Yeah, we saw you a few days ago. Are you camping nearby?"

He shrugged. "Here and there. Kind of checking out the area, I guess."

Colt shifted his weight. "Are you thinking of moving here?"

"I'm not sure. I guess it depends on what I find out while I'm here, and if I find what I'm looking for."

Kate gave the man her friendliest smile. "What are you looking for? Are you hoping to buy a house? It's a nice place to live." She cast a glance at her friends, then back at the man. "Do you like horses?"

He appeared startled at the change of topic. "Yeah. I guess so. But I've never ridden. They're kind of big, though."

Jake cleared his throat. "Exactly what I say. Big and fast and scary. Hey, did you know that someone's been letting horses—"

Kate saw Colt's elbow shoot out and catch Jake in the side. The younger boy grunted and bent over a bit, then straightened and glared. "What'd you do that for, Colt? All I was going to say was—"

"We know what you were going to say, Jake. This guy was going to tell us what he's looking for. He's not interested in local gossip."

"It's not gossip, it's—"

"Jake." Kate stared at him and raised her brows.

"What?" He adjusted his glasses, then his face reddened. "Oh. Right-o. Sorry. Yeah." He ran an invisible zipper along his closed lips.

The man stared from one face to the other. "Did I miss something? Is there a problem?"

Colt shook his head. "Nope. Not at all. My friend here gets a little excited sometimes, that's all. He loves old movies and TV shows, and sometimes he gets started on that subject and doesn't realize it's not the right time to talk about it. So you were saying?"

The dog whined and tugged at the leash. "Yes, Kenton, we'll go soon. You're probably getting hungry." The man reached down and stroked the dog's silky yellow fur, then looked up and seemed to hesitate. "Do you kids know an older lady named Martha? I don't know her last name—she may have remarried—but it could be Spencer."

Kate felt tingles run up her arms. Could he be talking about Mrs. Maynard? And if so, why was he looking for her? "What does she look like?"

He shook his head. "I have no idea. I've never seen her."

Colt bumped Kate's knee with his own and shot her a quick look. "Sorry, it's kind of hard to say if we know her. There are a lot of people in this area, even if it is rural. It would help if you could tell us her last name or something else about her."

"Or why you're looking for her," Tori blurted the words.

"Yeah," Melissa edged forward. "Why do you want to know?"

The man took a step back, and the dog gave a soft rumble deep in his throat. "Hey, don't worry about it. I'd rather not discuss it, know what I mean? Have a good ride." He lifted his hand in a salute and walked briskly away, his dog walking eagerly ahead of him.

Jake punched Colt lightly on the arm. "Hey—what was that elbow all about? And you guys do too know an older lady named Martha. Why didn't you tell him about Mrs. Maynard? I didn't say anything because she's your friend, but I don't get why you shut me up about the horses getting loose and didn't tell him anything. What's with all the secrecy?"

Melissa rolled her eyes. "Jake, Jake, Jake. It's very possible that guy is the one letting the horses out. He has a dog that looks exactly like the one in the picture, he's walking down the same road where several horses were let loose, and now he's asking questions about an older lady named Martha, and he wouldn't tell us why he wanted to know. Sorry, dude, but I agree with Colt and Kate about keeping quiet. If he's not going to tell us anything, we need to keep any information we have to ourselves. We can't be too careful."

"Right," Tori said. "I mean, he seems nice enough, and clean and nicely dressed, but you can't always tell by appearances. He could be trouble, and we need to be careful."

Jake twisted his lips to the side and narrowed his eyes behind his thick lenses. "So let's follow him. Put a tail on him. You know, like the detectives do that I was telling you about. Maybe we can't sit in a police car on a stakeout and eat donuts, but we could see where he's going and what he does, right?"

Kate wanted to laugh at the idea at first, but then she stopped. "You know, that might not be such a bad idea."

Jake grinned. "Cool! Awesome! Neato! We need to hang back a little so he doesn't notice us. You know, like on *Get Smart*, that old black-and-white spy show from the sixties. Now that was one funny show. They never did anything that was really smart, but somehow they managed to figure out who the bad guys were and catch them by the time the show was over. Most of the time they messed up or did something stupid, but they always got their man. Did you guys ever watch that show?"

Colt stared at Jake and slowly shook his head. "Nope. Never even heard of it." He glanced at Kate. "I'm not so sure that's a good idea. I can't see five kids following the guy down the road. He's walking. We'd catch him way too soon, and he'd notice. Besides, it's pretty obvious we were headed the opposite direction. Wouldn't it look suspicious to ride up behind him and tail him?"

Kate slapped her forehead. "Duh. Of course it would. Guess I wasn't thinking. So what now—just let it go?"

"Nope," Colt said. "We keep our eyes open, like Jake said. We need to be good detectives and watch for this guy. He might be totally harmless, but you never know. He could be up to no good, and he could be the one turning the horses loose. But until we see him again, we'd better keep trying to find Rebel's owner, and hope no other horses disappear from their pastures in the meantime."

CHAPTER TEN

KATE STOOD WITH TORI BY THE CORRAL FENCE, awed once again at Rebel's behavior with Pete. She could as easily say she was awed at Pete's behavior with Rebel. Her little brother was more demonstrative with the horse than he'd ever been with a member of their family. He murmured soft words she couldn't understand while he stroked the horse's face.

As for Rebel, he held perfectly still. The horse seemed to understand he shouldn't frighten the little boy, who appeared to be pouring out his heart in Rebel's ear.

Kate's mom had tried to snap a lead rope on the horse earlier today, but he had snorted and reared and dashed away. Mom had told Kate she would try again while Pete was reaching through the bars and caressing the horse. Now she approached him from inside the corral, on his left side.

Tori leaned close, her voice dropped to a whisper. "Your mom is closer to Rebel than she's ever been before. And he isn't even paying attention to her. It's like he's so focused on Pete that he doesn't care about anything else. Crazy, but so cool."

"Yeah." Kate drew back from the fence so Rebel wouldn't feel threatened then looked at her mother who had halted. "Mom, is everything okay?"

Her mother nodded but didn't reply. She eased closer to the big gelding, who kept his head lowered to allow Pete to scratch under his forelock. She paused then and said, "Have Pete give him a carrot if he starts to move."

Kate grinned. "His eyes are half-shut. I don't think he's going anywhere."

"Right. But remember what he did after you snapped on a lead rope last time. If he rears or strikes out, I want you to grab Pete and get him away from the fence. Move closer to Pete now. We can't be too careful."

Kate's pulse raced when she remembered the way Rebel had reacted when she'd caught him. Her guardian angel must have been working overtime that day, because she could have gotten kicked or worse. She shivered and rubbed her hands on her bare arms, even though it was a hot day. Maybe that was why Rebel was half asleep. No—it was definitely Pete's touch that made the big horse so calm.

"Please, God." She whispered the short prayer, not wanting anything bad to happen this time. Not only for her mom's sake, but so Pete wouldn't be scared, too.

Her mom moved to the horse's head, where she slowly reached over and clipped the lead rope to the ring on Rebel's halter. The gelding raised his head a few inches and looked at her, then lowered it again so Pete could continue stroking his face.

"Wow!" Tori gave a modified fist pump but kept her voice low. "You did it, Mrs. Ferris! Now what?"

"Kate, hand me a brush from your tack box." Her mother stayed close to the bars and kept her eyes on Pete and Rebel.

Kate did as instructed and held her breath as her mother started to groom the horse, staying clear of his hindquarters and back legs. "He's doing great. I don't think we'd want to see how he'd act if Pete was gone, though. I'm sure that's what's keeping him quiet."

"Yeah, this is the perfect test run. I can't believe how much that horse has bonded with Pete."

"Yeah, and the other way around, too." Kate gazed at her little brother, who was still in his own world—or his and Rebel's world, as the horse had moved a few inches closer, if that was possible. Rebel seemed to ignore Mom and her brush as she ran it over the rest of his body. "Are you going to try to brush out his mane? It's all tangled."

"Not this time—that might be pushing it. We'll do this again tomorrow and see how it goes, but I'm guessing it will get easier every time, as long as Pete is here."

The screen on the front door banged, and Dad came out in the yard. "Nan! You might want to take this call." He shielded his eyes against the sun's glare. "Or I can take the number and you can call them back. I forgot you were going in with the wild horse."

Kate's mom slowly unsnapped the lead and then headed toward the gate. "Who is it? I can be there in a minute if they don't mind waiting."

"They say they know who owns Rebel."

Kate's heart lurched—whether with excitement or disappointment, she wasn't sure. Pete had grown so attached to this horse that it would break his heart for Rebel to leave. She had started to secretly believe the owner would never be found, and maybe they could keep Rebel forever.

She pulled a carrot from her back pocket and squatted down beside Pete. "Hey, buddy. You can break this into pieces and give it to your friend if you want to. I'll stay right here."

He didn't take his eyes off Rebel, but his voice was strong. "Rebel is my friend. Rebel lives at our house, nowhere else. Rebel is mine."

Kate heard a soft gasp and knew Tori had heard. What would they do now? If only the horse could disappear when the owners came, and they could claim he'd run away again. But that wouldn't be right or honest, and no way would her parents—or God—approve. No, she'd simply have to pray that somehow her little brother would forget soon and not be hurt too deeply.

Kate watched in nervous anticipation when a car pulled into the parking area by their barn the next day. Tori, Melissa, Colt, and Jake all stood silently nearby. She had called them, knowing her friends wanted to be there when the owner arrived. After all the work they'd done to solve the mystery, what a letdown that they hadn't even found the person. Instead, someone had called her parents. Of course, the call came after Kate and her friends showed the photo at the different barns, so she guessed they'd had some part in it. But that didn't make her feel any better.

Colt leaned close to the girls, his voice low. "Kinda wish we hadn't shown the picture so much, know what I mean? This is going to hit Pete hard."

Melissa stood with her arms across her chest, and she heaved a deep sigh. "Not even M&M's will help make this better. Why couldn't they show up days ago, before Pete and Rebel got to be friends? It's hard losing something you love."

Kate slipped her hand through the crook of Melissa's arm and squeezed. She couldn't begin to imagine what it would be like to lose her dad and then have most of her friends desert her because they found out the popular girl wasn't rich after all. Sometimes life wasn't fair. "Sorry, Melissa."

Melissa squeezed her arm in return. "Yeah, but you know what? It's also awesome when God replaces what you lost with something as awesome as you guys."

The car door opened, and a short woman close to Kate's mom's age got out, followed by a teenage boy with shaggy hair and torn jeans who looked about Colt's age.

Kate's mom stepped forward and shook the woman's hand. "Hi!" She gestured at the group crowded around her now. "I'm Nan Ferris, this is my husband, John, and my daughter, Kate, and her friends. They've all been trying very hard to find Rebel's owner and get him back home." She touched Pete's head with a gentle hand. "And this is our youngest, Pete. He's managed to make friends with your horse while he's been here, and I'm afraid he'll be very sorry to see him leave."

"I'm Gloria Marks, but please call me Gloria." The woman glanced around at all the faces. "So you named him Rebel? I have to say that's better than his real name."

Her son gave a snort of laughter. "No kidding. Stupid horse."

"I'm sorry," Kate's mom said with a frown, "I'm not following. What's his name?"

Gloria arched a brow. "My son Kyle calls him Stupid, but his name is Bay. Not fancy, I know, but my husband wasn't a fancy person."

Kyle muttered something under his breath.

"What's that, son?" Kate's dad asked the boy.

"I said, my dad wasn't fancy or committed or trustworthy, or anything else. The horse was his. That's why I call him Stupid. My dad was stupid and so is the horse."

"Kyle!" Gloria glared at her son. "That's enough of that talk. These people aren't interested in our personal problems, and they've been kind enough to take care of Bay."

"Yeah, well, I don't really care." He turned and yanked open the door of the car, got in, and slammed it shut.

Gloria's face paled. "I'm so sorry. Please forgive my son. His dad left us a few weeks ago, not long after we moved here, and Kyle has been so angry. My ex always spent more time with that horse than he did his kids. Then he left the horse—and all of us."

Kate's mom put her arm around Gloria's shoulder and gave her a brief hug. "That's hard for all of you. Would you like to board Rebel—er—Bay here, instead of taking him home?"

Kate shot Tori a hopeful look. Maybe Pete wouldn't have to lose his new friend after all. If only the woman would say yes.

But Gloria shook her head. "No. But thank you. We have a small pasture. I don't know how he got out and made his way over here." She sighed. "I'm not sure how we'll get him home, though. Roger was the only person who could handle that horse, and it took him hours to coax him into a horse trailer."

"How far away do you live?" Kate's dad asked.

"Not far. We're only a mile down the road, but we're almost a quarter mile up a private driveway that's kind of overgrown with brush and weeds. That might be why your kids didn't make it to our house when they were searching. Plus, I'm afraid I haven't been paying attention to the horse the past couple of weeks. The kids were supposed to be making sure Bay had water in his tank. He had plenty of grass to eat, but I found out Kyle wasn't keeping up on the water. That might be why Bay got out. I'm sorry I didn't notice sooner. Can I pay you for your trouble and whatever you had to feed him?" Her face crumpled into worry lines that had carved deep grooves in her face.

Dad shot a glance at Mom, and they both shook their heads at the same time. "That isn't necessary at all," Mom said. "It wasn't enough to fuss over. And that isn't very far to lead him. Would you want to do that instead of trying to deal with a trailer?"

Mrs. Marks shuddered. "No! I won't touch that horse. He doesn't like me, and I've never been much of a horse person. We'll figure out a way."

Kate touched her dad's arm. "How about if Mom and I walk him over? I think if Pete is with us, Rebel will be fine. She led him around in the corral this morning before Mrs. Marks came, and he did great with Pete in the center of the ring." She grinned. "I mean, he kept wanting to come to the center so Pete could pet him, but he didn't cause any trouble."

Her dad raised his brows. "Nan? Is that something you'd be willing to do?"

Mom gave a slow nod. "Yes, I think so. Kate's right. With Pete along, Rebel should be fine." She turned to Mrs. Marks. "How is he with cars? Is it apt to spook him if one goes by while we're leading him?"

"I don't think so. My husband—" She cringed and started over. "My ex-husband rode him in parades and took him to play days. He never gave him a problem."

"All right." Mom pushed a curl of hair from her eyes. "Does tomorrow work for you? I don't have time to bring him over today, unless you really need me to."

Mrs. Marks gave what sounded like a relieved sigh. "Tomorrow is great, thank you. I hope you won't mind if I don't stay any longer. I work full-time, and I have a part-time job as a waitress besides, and that job starts in an hour. I need to get home and change. I'll look for you around this time tomorrow, if that's okay with you."

Pete let out a wail and plopped down on the ground. Kate had completely forgotten him while they'd been talking to Mrs. Marks. She knelt down beside him. "What's wrong, buddy?"

He continued to wail and pulled away when she tried to touch him. She could only make out one thing between cries. "Rebel. Rebel. Rebel."

Kate's heart began to break.

CHAPTER ELEVEN

THE NEXT DAY, KATE MET UP with her friends at her barn, trying her best to shove down the anger and tears she'd been holding in since delivering Rebel to his real home. Why hadn't God helped her little brother? It didn't seem fair to allow a horse to show up at their place and let her brother get so attached, only to take the horse away again.

She didn't understand everything about the way God worked, but sometimes He didn't make sense to her. And heaven seemed like a long way off to figure it all out. She sighed. There was nothing she could do about it, so it was probably better to let it go and not stay upset—even if that was easier to say than to do.

She scuffed her foot against a clump of weeds and wildflowers. "Hey, would you guys pray for Pete? He's having a hard time with Rebel being gone."

"Sure," said Colt, while Melissa nodded and Tori gave Kate a quick hug. "Poor little kid," Tori said. "It's tough to fall in love with an animal and then lose it."

"I wish we could've done something to make it better," Colt said. "Speaking of making things better, I think we need to watch out for Mrs. Maynard. We don't want her getting hurt."

Kate perked up, thankful for the change in subject, but grateful to know her friends would pray. "Why, what's up?"

He plunked down on a bale of straw under a tree and stuck a piece between his teeth. "I rode over on my bike, and I saw that guy again."

Jake jumped up from where he'd sat. "The one with the dog?" His voice broke into a high note in excitement. "Sheesh! I sounded like a girl. And no, I don't have a movie comment for that one."

All of them laughed, and Melissa tugged him back down. "Sit, Jake. It's too hot to stand around." She turned to Colt. "Where did you see him? Walking along the road again?"

"Nope. You remember, where we went through the woods and came out on the pasture hillside, and we could see her back door?"

Tori shivered. "When she came outside and waved her rifle at us. I'm still thankful she didn't try to shoot us."

Jake peered from one to the other. "How come I haven't heard this part of the story? All I know about is her horse."

"We'd better save it for another time," Tori said. "We probably need to hear what Colt has to say. Sounds like it's important."

"Right," Jake agreed. "Proceed, Colt. Continue, move on, resume." He grinned. "You get the point."

Colt laughed. "Yep. I got it back at 'right.' So anyway, I was riding over here, and I saw somebody disappear in the brush on that path leading to Mrs. Maynard's place. I parked my bike and followed him for a few yards, and I could see the dog and the guy moving real slow and peeking through the trees and brush."

Melissa gasped. "Did he see you following him?"

"Nope. He started to turn around at one point, so I hit the ground and stayed down for a long time. When I got up, he'd disappeared. Guess I should be glad the dog didn't bark or come sniff me out. I was pushing my luck following him."

"What's he doing spying on Mrs. Maynard?" Tori sat up straight, indignation clouding her face. "She's our friend. She's been harassed enough in the past. We can't let anything happen to her."

"I agree," Kate said, "but we don't know for sure he's spying on her. He said he's new to the area, so maybe he just thought he found a shortcut through the woods or wanted to explore."

Melissa pursed her lips. "Or he was hoping to find a good camping spot."

"Right." Colt nodded. "But don't you think we should check it out? What if he is spying on her? We don't know this guy, and he might be some escaped criminal for all we know. Dressing in nice clothes doesn't mean anything."

"Yeah," Jake said. "There's a ton of documentaries about criminals who don't seem like criminals at first. Not that I ever watch those. My parents draw the line at real life stuff that's about crime. But I've heard them mention it. And I've seen stories on the news about someone getting caught, and all the neighbors say they never would've guessed 'cause he was such a nice guy."

"You guys are creeping me out." Tori rubbed her hands on her bare arms. "Do you really think Mrs. Maynard could be in danger? We need to warn her. Shouldn't we go over there right now?"

Colt pushed to his feet. "Will your parents care if we all ride over and check on her, Kate? We could ride down her regular driveway, then casually ask if she's seen anybody snooping around."

"Yeah, but we don't want to scare her," Melissa said. "She's getting old, you know, and she lives alone. What if we give her a heart attack by telling her?"

Kate shook her head. "She's a very strong lady. I think we can ask a few questions without causing any trouble. And maybe we could poke around in the back pasture and see if the guy is camping there. We could tell Mrs. Maynard there's a guy with a dog and a sleeping bag who cut through the woods behind her place, and we want to make sure he isn't camping. He could start a fire and burn down the woods."

"Agreed." Colt headed for his bike. "Want to check with your parents, Kate?"

"Yep. Give me a second." She raced for the house and returned quickly. "Mom said it's fine. She feels bad 'cause we've been so busy with other things that we've neglected Mrs. Maynard and Mr. Wallace." She held up a brown paper bag. "She put two baggies of cookies in here. We're supposed to drop one by Mr. Wallace's house and give the other one to Mrs. Maynard."

"All right!" Jake pumped his fist in the air. "Cookies! Energy for the road. Nutrition. Sustenance for our bodies. I'm in heaven now."

Melissa smacked him lightly on the shoulder. "Forget it, Jake. These are for our friends, not for us. You'll be lucky if

Mrs. Maynard offers us one, and even if she does, we shouldn't take any. There are five of us and only one of her. We can't eat all her cookies."

"Oh." He slumped, and the miserable expression on his face made them all laugh. "Do you think your mom could spare one for each of us, Kate? Pretty please? It's been forever since I had any sugar. I think I'm expiring. Wasting away. Shriveling up. Seriously."

Kate caught her breath to keep from laughing. Jake was too funny, and he acted like he meant it. "I think she could manage to share, but let's wait and make it our treat for when we return. We really should get going. Mrs. Maynard's safety is more important than our stomachs."

The kids coasted their bikes to a halt fifteen minutes later in front of Mrs. Maynard's house. Kate knew it was fifteen minutes because Jake had set the timer function on his watch, determined to know exactly how long the trip would take. He claimed if he had to go more than an hour without food, he'd probably die. Or expire, as he'd put it. She tried not to snicker.

She really liked Jake, but he still took some getting used to. She blew out her breath as they all parked their bikes, hoping Mrs. Maynard was fine.

Parked on the grass, they all looked at one another, and no one moved. Kate swatted at a pesky fly. "I guess we should have talked about what we'd say before we got here. We don't want to scare her. Do we pretend we only came to visit and drop off cookies, or—"

A voice came from the back corner of the house. "Why would you need to pretend? So you didn't come to visit or bring cookies?" Mrs. Maynard's wrinkled face was lit by a soft smile, but her hands were planted on her hips in a no-nonsense gesture.

Tori rushed to the older woman and wrapped her arms around her shoulders in a quick hug. "Of course, we came to visit! We love coming to see you." She waved toward Kate. "And yes, we brought cookies. Mrs. Ferris sent them."

"Ah, so what was all that I heard about pretending? Is something going on that I need to know about?" She tucked her hand through the crook of Tori's arm and led her back toward Kate and her friends.

Melissa cleared her throat and looked from one to the other. "Well, there might be. That is, we aren't exactly sure."

Jake answered in a high-pitched chirp. "We think someone might be spying on you."

Colt groaned and grabbed Jake around the neck in a friendly headlock. "Jake! We were going to think about what to say, not just blurt it out." He released Jake with a grin. "Sorry for grabbing you. But hey, you might be the only one with any smarts. We do need to be honest with Mrs. Maynard."

Jake grinned. "My brother Jerry grabs me all the time, but he does a lot worse than that, so it's cool." His glasses had slipped clear to the tip of his nose, so he shoved them up. "But watch the specs after this, huh? Mom will kill me if I break another pair and she has to replace them again. The next pair will come out of my allowance. Not good. Horrible, in fact. Awful. Atrocious—"

Colt held out his arm, and Jake ducked. "Right. Got it. Time to be quiet. Yep. No problem." He clamped his hand over his mouth. "Sorry."

Colt laughed, and even Mrs. Maynard joined in. She raised her brows and faced Kate. "So, cookies first, and then you can explain why you came to visit and why you think someone might be spying on me."

Kate pulled a plastic baggie of cookies out of the sack. "The others are for Mr. Wallace. We'll drop them off on the way home."

"Ah, yes. Mr. Wallace. That's very kind of you children." She took the baggie and her eyes widened. "Oh my! Are those your mother's famous apple-raisin-nut cookies? The last time I had these, I thought I'd died and gone to heaven."

Jake edged closer. "Apple and raisin and nuts? Yum." He clapped his hand over his mouth again. "Oops. Sorry. Again."

Mrs. Maynard looked at him, her forehead wrinkling. "Why be sorry, dear? You didn't say anything wrong."

Jake removed his hand. "Because the guys told me not to ask for a cookie, since you wouldn't have enough to share with everyone, and we didn't want to make you feel bad. But now I've probably made you feel bad. So I'm sorry again. Truly. For sure. Absolutely." He sighed. "There I go again. I can't seem to stop doing that."

Mrs. Maynard laughed. "I think it's delightful. So many young people nowadays have no vocabulary at all. They can only use words with one syllable or no meaning." She held up the baggie and inspected it again. "I'd say there are at least two dozen cookies in here. More than enough for all of us. Come in the house so I can pour each of us a glass of milk or water. Then we'll eat our cookies and you can tell me what's going on."

CHAPTER TWELVE

WHILE THEY ATE COOKIES WITH Mrs. Maynard in her kitchen, Kate explained what they suspected about the man they'd seen, as well as what Colt had seen earlier that day.

Mrs. Maynard listened carefully, nodding occasionally. "So you think he could be camping in the woods above my back pasture? I don't suppose that would be so terrible, would it? You said he looks like a nice young man?"

Kate exchanged a glance with Colt, then her gaze shot around the room to each of her friends, seeing looks of encouragement, concern, and even something close to fear on Tori's face. She plunged forward. "Well, I think what made us worry is that he's asking if anyone knows an older lady in the area whose first name is Martha. Then he snuck down the path to the woods behind your place, so we kind of figured he might be dangerous."

Mrs. Maynard dipped her head and didn't speak for a moment. Finally, she raised her head and peered at each of them in turn. "I appreciate that you care about an old lady, but I doubt I'm in any danger. Although it is too hot for anyone to camp and start a fire. He should probably stay in a campground and not be sleeping on private property. Are you thinking we should walk back there and see if he's pitched a tent?"

Colt took a final drink of his milk and set his glass on a coaster on a nearby table. "Yes, ma'am, that's exactly what we were thinking. But you don't need to walk all the way up there. We can go check it out, then come down and let you know if we found him and what he said."

"Certainly not, young man." She got to her feet. "I may have my share of wrinkles, but I'm not too old to take a walk up through the pasture to the woods. In fact, I'd enjoy it. If you're all finished, let's go. There's no sense in waiting or discussing it any longer." She headed to the door then glanced over her shoulder. "Well, are you all going to sit there, or are you coming with me?"

The five of them sprang to their feet and raced across the room and out the door. Kate couldn't believe how fast Mrs. Maynard could walk. Of course, she'd gotten a head start, but they had to break into a jog to catch up. Kate slowed beside the older woman. "What will you say if he's there? Will you tell him he needs to leave?"

Mrs. Maynard smiled. "I don't know, dear. I suppose it depends on what he says when we speak to him. Let's wait and see, shall we?"

"He has a big dog." Kate wasn't sure why she'd blurted out the information. "It's a golden retriever. But it's friendly. Or at least, it was the one time we came close."

"That's good." She smiled again and kept walking.

When they reached the edge of the woods they moved more slowly, picking their way around brush and over small fallen logs and branches that must have come down in a windstorm. Colt stretched out a hand to steady Mrs. Maynard as she stepped over a downed tree. They got about halfway through the woods to where the path exited on the road.

Kate paused and looked every direction. "I don't see anybody. Do you think he came and left already?"

"Look!" Jake rushed forward. "It looks like someone's been camping here." He bent over and parted a large clump of brush. "There's a rolled up sleeping bag here and a tarp. No tent, though."

Colt peered under the branches. "He must be trying to hide it. He might even be a criminal. So now what? Do we wait till he comes back and tell him to get lost? Or should we call the sheriff and let him know somebody's trespassing?"

Mrs. Maynard shook her head. "Neither one. Leaving a tarp and sleeping bag under a bush isn't a crime. We have no proof he's staying here. There's no sign of a campfire. In fact, we don't know for sure this even belongs to the man you saw earlier. I see no sense in causing trouble for anyone who hasn't done a thing wrong that we're aware of."

Tori moved close to Mrs. Maynard. "But we can't leave without knowing you're safe. What if he comes back tonight and sleeps here?"

She laughed. "I hardly think that's a threat. He's way up here in the woods. I have a tightly locked house and a telephone, if anyone tries to break in." She rested a hand on Colt's shoulder. "And Colt's family lives just up the road. What if I promise to call his father if anything suspicious happens? Will you children feel good about going home then?"

They exchanged glances, and Kate nodded. "Maybe. If you promise."

Mrs. Maynard made an X over her chest. "Cross my heart. Better now?"

Colt broke a dead branch off a nearby tree and snapped it in half. "I'm still worried."

"Tell you what. How about you children ride your bikes back over here in the morning, first thing. Don't come in this way, come to the house. We'll all walk up here again and see if he's here."

Melissa wrapped her arms around herself and shivered. "Okay. But we think he may be the one who's letting horses out around the area. We don't know why he'd be doing it, but it's possible he's a criminal. Maybe Colt should bring his dad with him, or Kate could bring Mr. Ferris."

"No, dear. I don't think that's necessary. Let's talk to the young man first. I doubt he's going to tackle an old woman and five children. There's nothing he'd have to gain by doing that. We'll give him a chance to explain before we bring in anyone else. We can always ask him nicely to not camp here, and if he doesn't listen, then it might be time to bring in one of your parents."

Tori frowned. "Or the sheriff."

Forty-five minutes later, after walking Mrs. Maynard back to her house and talking it all through again with no change in

Mrs. Maynard's decision, they rode their bikes down the road to Kate's home. Colt led the group, with Jake beside him, Melissa and Tori side-by-side, and Kate bringing up the rear. She didn't mind. She wanted to think. Had she been too quick to rush into judging the stranger and assuming he was bad, simply because he carried a backpack and sleeping bag? Homeless people were slowly starting to come into the Hood River area, and she couldn't help but worry when she saw them begging at an overpass exit. But maybe she should wait and find out this man's story before she assumed the worst.

Then again, what if he was bad, and they had ignored him and hadn't brought him to Mrs. Maynard's attention? She could end up hurt, or worse. Relief hit Kate hard when they rounded the final corner and her barn came into sight. She suddenly hit her brakes and yelped.

Dust rose as four sets of bike tires skidded. "What's going on, Kate? Did you crash?" Tori brought her bike to a stop and turned a worried face her way.

Kate could only point and gasp. "Look! I can't believe it."

Rebel pranced in the area between the barn and the corral where he'd been kept, his coat gleaming in the afternoon sun. He gave a loud whinny, and the back door opened and slammed shut. Kate's mom came out, holding Pete's hand.

Pete shook off his mother's grip and raced forward. "Rebel! You came back. Rebel—my friend!"

Kate watched in horror as he ran straight for Rebel's front legs. Her mother seemed frozen in shock, then she suddenly bolted forward, but she was too far behind Pete to grab him before he got to the horse. If only she and her friends were closer! But racing up on their bikes would only spook the gelding, and Pete could get hurt.

"Pete," her mother called. "Don't go any closer. Wait for Mom."

Pete stopped and held out his hand. Rebel snorted and lowered his head, sniffing at the little boy's hand. The big horse took another step, then nudged Pete's shoulder and lowered his head even further. Pete reached out and stroked Rebel's face, rubbing his favorite spot under his forelock.

Kate propped her bike against a corral rail. She could swear the horse had his eyes shut in pure pleasure. Where was the animal that had nearly killed her the day he'd arrived? How had he changed into this puppy-like creature?

Pete, she thought—*that's how.* Her little brother seemed to have a magic touch where Rebel was concerned. And more than likely, Pete's guardian angel was standing next to the horse and whispering in his ear.

Kate shook her head in amazement, never dreaming this could happen. "Mom, how long has he been here? What's going on?" She parked her bike and waited for her friends to join her, then they walked slowly and quietly toward her mother.

Nan's eyes were wide with surprise—and probably shock. "I heard a noise outside and thought maybe one of our horses had gotten out. Pete insisted on coming. He said it was 'his Rebel.' I told him no, Rebel was at his own home now, but he wanted to come with me. The minute Pete saw Rebel, he took off running. I'm sure you saw the rest. Amazing. Scary, but amazing. I don't know what to make of it." She walked up to Pete and touched his shoulder. "Son, let's see if we can get Rebel to go into the corral, okay? Maybe Tori could go in the house and get carrots."

Tori sprinted for the house.

Melissa edged closer to Pete. "How did Rebel get loose this time? Do you think the same people let him out? Maybe we should call the sheriff again."

Mom brushed the hair from her eyes. "No, I don't think so. I'll call Gloria first. Maybe she can shed some light on what happened. No sense in worrying anyone until we know the facts." She withdrew her phone from her hip pocket. "Kate, before I call, would you please come stand by your brother?

Rebel looks like he's nearly asleep, but I'd rather have someone next to Pete in case he suddenly wakes up and decides to cause trouble." She waited until Kate stood next to Pete before she dialed. "Mrs. Marks? Hi, it's Nan Ferris." She waited a moment, listening. "Yes. He's here. Do you know how he got out?" She paused again. "Okay, right—would you like us to walk him over again? My husband isn't home, so once we get there, do you think you could run Pete and me home?" She waited a moment. "Thanks. We'll be there in thirty minutes or so." She hit the off button and slipped the phone back in her pocket.

"How'd he get out?" Kate asked. "Does she think it was the same kids?"

"No. She said Rebel has been reaching over the gate and worrying the latch with his lips and teeth ever since we brought him home. She thinks he opened the gate and let himself out. Hard to believe, I know."

Jake grinned. "Like I said before, exactly like Mr. Ed the talking horse. There are a ton of smart horses, though. It's not that unusual for a horse to escape a pen or pasture. They can jump out, or open a gate, or all sorts of things. Pretty smart horse if you ask me. He sure must love Pete."

Kate's eyes widened. "No kidding! And how is the Marks family going to keep him home if he decides he wants to run away again?"

CHAPTER THIRTEEN

KATE, TORI, AND COLT RODE TO Mrs. Maynard's the next day without Melissa and Jake. Both of their parents had chores for them to do, and the only reason Tori's mom hadn't kept her home was because Tori convinced her that helping Mrs. Maynard was the right thing to do. After all, how could she say no when the older lady was the reason Tori now had her own horse?

Kate was thrilled that at least two of her friends had been able to come. She'd hate for her and Mrs. Maynard to go up in the woods and run into that stranger. Not that she wouldn't be brave enough, but being surrounded by friends was comforting.

Tori nudged her after they parked their bikes against Mrs. Maynard's fence. "Are you scared?" She kept her voice low so Colt couldn't hear. It hadn't been long ago that Tori struggled with overcoming her fears in more than one area. Kate was proud of Tori for agreeing to come today.

Kate gave a half nod. "I guess a little. But I think Mrs. Maynard is right. That guy isn't going to attack an old lady and a bunch of kids. At least, he didn't seem like the kind of person who would."

"But you never know about people. We're supposed to stay away from strangers, right?" Tori pressed her lips together.

"Right. When we're on our own. We have an adult with us, so we need to trust she knows what she's doing."

Tori sighed. "I'm trusting God that He'll take care of us. He's a lot bigger and stronger than Mrs. Maynard."

Colt came up behind them and placed a gentle hand on each of their shoulders. "Quit worrying, girls. You have me, God, and Mrs. Maynard to watch out for you. What more could you want?"

"Jake!" Kate and Tori spoke at the same time, and all three erupted in laughter.

Kate tried to contain her giggles. "Jake would entertain the guy with his movie references, and he'd forget why he came to cause trouble."

Colt rolled his eyes. "Girls! I think I finally have you figured out, and you come up with something like that. Let's go see if Mrs. Maynard is ready."

They trooped to the door and knocked, but no one answered. When they walked around the house to the backyard, they found Mrs. Maynard standing on the small covered porch, a pair of binoculars to her eyes, trained up the hill toward the woods.

"Hey, Mrs. M.," Kate called out.

She lowered her binoculars. "Hello, children. I've been watching off and on for the past hour, and I haven't seen any sign of our visitor. He may have packed up and left last night or early this morning."

Colt groaned. "I was hoping we'd get a chance to talk to the guy. Do you still want to walk up and check it out, just in case?"

She pressed her lips together, then nodded. "Yes, I suppose that would be best. I put on my walking shoes in case we decided to trek up through the pasture." She got a dreamy look in her eyes. "So many wonderful hours spent sitting and watching Starlight play in this pasture." She focused her gaze on Tori. "I'm so glad you're caring for him, dear. It gives me a great sense of relief, although I do occasionally miss seeing him out here." She waved her hand toward the gently sloping hillside.

Tori snuggled close to the older woman, giving her a side-hug. "You need to come visit Starlight more. He's always so happy to see you."

"Yes, well." Mrs. Maynard swiped her fingers under her eyes. "Enough of that. We need to take care of the business at hand. Let's go see what we can discover about this stranger who's been haunting my woods and asking questions about me. I'm very curious what he's up to and what motivated him to come to our little town."

The four of them spent the next thirty minutes walking up the hill and scouring the woods, but they didn't find any sign of the intruder. Mrs. Maynard planted her hands on her hips as they stood at the edge of the woods. "I'd say we've looked in every nook and cranny big enough to hide a grown man—or a small child, for that matter. It appears he's disappeared again. I'm guessing he's simply a transient who was looking for a safe place to sleep for the night, and now he's gone. We shouldn't waste any more time or worry on what might have been. Time to head back to the house. I still have a few of those cookies you brought yesterday."

Kate felt like a balloon that suddenly had all the air released in a whoosh—flat and spent. Part of her was relieved they didn't have to confront the man, while the other part was disappointed they wouldn't solve this most recent mystery.

Would the man disappear, and they'd never know what he was up to? Or would he suddenly turn up again, spying on Mrs. Maynard and possibly causing her harm? What could he want with an old lady who lived alone on a quiet country road? And why sneak around and not come out and ask whatever he wanted to know? She didn't like this one bit.

Suddenly a bark sounded in the distance, and Kate's ears perked up. Could that be the man's golden retriever? Were they coming back, or had he somehow snuck off and avoided being seen by Mrs. Maynard and her binoculars earlier?

Colt froze, his arm raised in a gesture of quiet. None of them moved for several long minutes, but the bark wasn't repeated. "Could you ladies tell where that came from? Was it close, or far away?"

Mrs. Maynard cocked her head to the side. "My hearing isn't what it used to be, so I can't say. Girls?"

Tori twisted her lips to the side in a look of concentration. "Far away, I think. But I'm not sure either. Do we hang out here a while longer and see if he comes back?" She hugged herself, her eyes wide.

Kate sighed. "I don't think so. The man is probably gone. The way things are going lately, I'm not sure we'll ever solve either mystery." She sighed, wondering if they should give up and quit trying. Then something her father said in the past straightened her spine. With God's help they could do all things—nothing was too hard if you asked and believed. "But maybe if we keep praying, God will help us figure it out. And we should pray for Him to keep Mrs. Maynard safe, too."

The rest of the day dragged by for Kate. Tori and Colt had to go home, and Pete moped and cried for Rebel, refusing to be comforted. Kate hurt for her little brother. He didn't understand why his friend, as he called him, couldn't stay at their house forever, especially after the horse had returned the day before.

Poor Mrs. Marks had been pretty upset too, when they'd taken Rebel back and put him in his pasture again. She told them she planned to have Kyle check the entire fence line and make sure it wasn't down anywhere along the pasture boundaries, as well as secure the gate latch to make sure Rebel wouldn't escape again. Keeping him cooped up in a stall all the time wasn't the answer, and Mrs. Marks didn't want to buy more hay when she had perfectly good pasture grass that Rebel could be eating.

Kate plopped down on the couch next to her mother and brother. Mom was rocking Pete, who had fallen into a restless sleep. It was the only time the little guy allowed anyone to hold him, and Kate knew her mom took any chance she could to cuddle him.

"Hey, Mom?" she whispered.

"Yes?" Her mother seemed distracted, like she was listening with her ears but not her mind.

Kate waited a minute, wondering if she should say anything. "Do you think Mrs. Maynard is safe living alone? Should we try to talk her into moving somewhere else?"

Mom focused her attention on Kate with the intensity of a bright light shining into a dark room—and it almost made Kate cringe. Almost, but not quite, since she cared so much about Mrs. Maynard. "Why would you say that?" Mom asked. "Is this about the man you saw walking with the dog? You told me he isn't hanging around any longer, so why are you worried?"

Kate bit her lip. "I'm not sure. It's more of a feeling that I can't explain. There's something really mysterious about that guy. I think he's hiding something, but I don't have any idea what. He seemed like a pretty nice guy when he talked to us."

She hesitated, struggling to explain something she wasn't sure she understood. "Maybe I'm crazy or imagining things, and he's not a bad man. Maybe he isn't after Mrs. Maynard at all. And maybe he's not the one who's been letting the horses out. But what if I'm wrong, and he's all of those things?"

CHAPTER FOURTEEN

A COUPLE OF DAYS LATER, KATE breathed a sigh of relief that nothing bad had happened since she had talked to her mom, despite her concerns. She lightly elbowed Tori in the arm and grinned. "I guess we were worried for nothing, huh?"

Tori bent over the pile of shavings and horse droppings she was ready to scoop into her wheelbarrow. "I was concentrating on beating Colt and Melissa in cleaning their stalls so we could ride. What's up?"

Colt hollered from the next stall. "Yeah, what are you talking about, Kate? And how come you're in Tori's stall? No fair helping someone else."

Kate laughed as Melissa's voice echoed the same sentiment one stall past Colt's. It was beyond cool that three of her four friends kept their horses at her parents' barn. Of course, Jake didn't own a horse and had no plans to ever get one.

She moved into the alleyway that ran between the stalls and the large indoor arena so everyone could hear her answer. "I'm not helping. I got my work done before you guys showed up. I've been hanging out with Jake while all of you work, but I thought I'd tell Tori that all our worry didn't amount to anything."

Colt stepped into the alleyway and leaned on his manure rake. "I didn't know you were worried. About what?"

"Yeah." Melissa poked her head out the door of her stall. "You never mentioned anything. How come we didn't get to worry with you?"

Kate laughed at that question. It had never occurred to her that someone might *want* to worry. "About Mrs. Maynard. Nothing bad has happened, and I'm very grateful. I guess the guy must have gone away. Rebel hasn't shown up here again, and no more horses have disappeared, so it looks like we're stuck with a boring summer again. Although I wish we'd solved the mysteries."

Tori grimaced. "We solved one of them—who owned Rebel—and he got to go back home. That's something, at least."

"Yeah," Kate said. "But then we still ended up with two more—why that man was asking about Mrs. Maynard and spying on her, and who let the horses out in the first place. Have any of you seen the man and his dog lately?"

Jake poked his head into the stall. "Yep. Saw him on the way over here today. Forgot to tell you." He slapped his forehead. "Man. Can't believe I did that. Not smart."

"Hey, you're telling us now and that's what matters." Colt gave Jake a playful shove. "Don't beat yourself up over it. So where did you see him? Anywhere near the trail that goes into the back of Mrs. Maynard's place?"

Jake made a face. "Let me think. Mouse and I decided to walk over and cheer Pete up."

"Hold it." Melissa held up her hand. "Mouse? Your dog? Where is he? You didn't bring him to the barn."

Jake grinned. "Nope. He and Rufus are in the back yard with Pete, playing in the kiddie pool. Mrs. Ferris is keeping an eye on them."

Melissa reached into her bike basket and pulled out a crumpled package of Peanut M&M's. "I had the same idea. Pete's been so sad lately, I thought these might help a little. I was going to give them to him when I finished my stall, before we took off on our ride. I guess they'd get wet if I took them back there now." She shoved them into her pocket. "That's awfully tempting right now, but something cold to drink sounds better."

Kate blew out a hard breath. "Yeah. Let's hurry up and finish our stalls. I'll help Tori finish, then we can help Colt and Melissa."

Colt laughed. "There's no way the two of you will finish before I do. You girls better move faster." He bolted back into his stall, and Kate could hear the sound of his pitchfork on the cement floor.

Kate cut a look at Jake. "Want to help, Jake? When we're done, I'll go grab us some pop, and you can tell us about the guy and his dog."

He pointed at his new sneakers. "No way am I going to take a chance of stepping in something squishy. My mom would shoot me! But I can push the wheelbarrow out and dump it on the pile when anyone is done."

They all returned to their work and finished quickly. A few minutes later, they gathered in Kate's backyard. Kate and Tori brought an assortment of cold drinks from the kitchen. Pete had climbed out of the wading pool and was wrapped in a towel and sitting between the two big dogs, crooning softly to Mouse.

Tori plunked down on a nearby blanket under a maple tree. "I can't get over how huge that dog is. And it still doesn't make sense why you'd name a Saint Bernard 'Mouse,' Jake. Why not 'Moose'? That fits him better."

"Nope. He's afraid of mice, remember?" Jake rolled his eyes behind his thick lenses. "So I called him that to encourage him to get past his fear."

Melissa chuckled. "Did it work?"

"Afraid not. But maybe someday." Jake sighed. "He's only a big puppy, you know. He won't be a year old for a few more months, and he won't get his full growth—or courage—until he's at least two. I still have hope."

Kate's mom smiled. "And you should, Jake. Don't let these four tease you. Pete loves Mouse, don't you, Pete?"

The little boy leaned his cheek against Mouse's head. "Mouse is my friend." He looked up, and tears glistened in his eyes. "Pete misses Rebel."

Kate sat next to Pete and the dogs and barely touched her brother's shoulder. "We know you do, buddy. But Rebel needed to live at his own home. His family would miss him too, if he stayed here." She wasn't sure that was exactly true, after the way Kyle had talked about the horse—and Mrs. Marks had seemed afraid of him. She'd wondered more than once if returning him was the right thing to do for Rebel's sake, but what choice did they have? He wasn't their horse, and it wasn't up to them to decide where he lived or what happened in his life, even though Pete longed for a different result. "So, Jake. Fill us in."

Her mother leaned forward. "On what? Did I miss something?"

Jake nodded. "I saw that man and his dog on the way over here today. I've been trying to remember where I saw them, and it finally came to me." He paused, and his lips pressed together in concentration.

Colt waved his hand in the air. "So spill it. Where did you see him?"

"It wasn't at the trail going into Mrs. Maynard's back woods or pasture."

"Good." Colt shifted the piece of straw in his mouth to the other side. "Come on, spit it out. Where'd you see him?"

Jake looked from one face to another. "At the end of the driveway going into the front of her house."

CHAPTER FIFTEEN

KATE JUMPED TO HER FEET, HER soda and tiredness forgotten. "Oh my gosh, Jake! Why did you take so long to tell us? Was he going up the driveway? Did it look like he was sneaking around and trying to stay out of sight?" She spun around and stared at her mother. "What if he's going to Mrs. Maynard's house to hurt her or steal something? We need to get over there and check on her, or at least warn her—if it's not already too late."

The rest of her friends also got to their feet, each one with a worried expression, and all gazes turned to Kate's mom.

Nan placed her finger to her lips and nodded toward Pete. The little boy's face crumpled like he was going to cry as he stared at Kate. "How about everyone sit down again, and keep your voices a bit lower?" she said. "We're scaring Pete." She waited until they all complied. "Now, exactly what did you see, Jake?"

He bit his lip. "Hmm… I remember the man and his dog were standing at the end of Mrs. Maynard's driveway, looking at her mailbox. He didn't move or anything, just stood there like he wasn't sure where he was or what he wanted to do. I was riding my bike, so I went by him pretty fast, but I slowed down before I got to the corner and looked back. He was still standing there. He didn't seem like he was in a rush to head up her driveway. I'll bet he was only resting, and he probably walked on up the road. Or maybe he went to his camping spot. I'm a pretty good detective, and I didn't see anything that made me suspicious. That's why I didn't tell you sooner. I kind of forgot about it."

Kate relaxed her tense posture and leaned back on her hands. "I guess it doesn't sound too bad. But Mom," she glanced at her mother, "could you call Mrs. Maynard and make sure she's okay? She'll probably think we're silly to ask, but I'm worried." Her gaze moved around her circle of friends.

Her mother set down the towel. "I don't see a problem with that. I'll go in and grab the phone. I meant to bring it out here but forgot."

The shrill sound of the home phone ringing in the kitchen set Kate's heart beating fast. She bolted to her feet and ran. "I'll get it." She tossed the words over her shoulder as she dashed into the kitchen, snatched the receiver out of the cradle, and headed back outside. "Ferris residence."

"Hello, dear. This is Martha Maynard. I was wondering if you and the other children might want to come over for a few minutes. And your mother, too, if she's home and would care to come. There's someone I'd like you all to meet."

Kate handed the phone to her mother and stood without moving as she tried to figure out exactly who and what Mrs. Maynard had meant. The older lady had asked for her mother right after she'd given the invitation to come over, but Kate could get little information from her mother's brief replies or from her lack of expression. Finally, she gave a quick nod. "Certainly. But it's going to be a large group of us. Are you sure you don't mind? Jake brought his dog, Mouse, and with John gone, I can't leave Pete alone. There's no way Kate will agree to stay to watch him." She winked at Kate.

Kate made a face. Stay here and watch Pete while everyone else went to Mrs. Maynard's? What if that man and his dog were there, putting her up to the phone call? No, that wasn't likely to be the case. If he was a bad guy, he wouldn't want her to invite a houseful of people over while he was there. So what could she possibly mean about someone she wanted them to meet?

Mom grinned. "Exactly what I expected—Kate wants to come. So I guess you're stuck with all of us, if you're sure that's all right?" She waited a moment then spoke. "I'll bring cookies. Coffee and lemonade sound wonderful. We'll be there in a few minutes, Martha."

All five of the kids stared at Kate's mom as she clicked off the phone and slipped it into her pocket. "My, aren't you all a bunch of eager beavers. I suppose you want to know what she said."

Each of them stared at her, their gazes' intent.

"Not a thing beyond what she told Kate. She said she has someone she'd like us to meet, but she wouldn't say who it was or why she wants all of us there, so I'm still as much in the dark as you are." She stood and gestured toward Pete. "How about you girls take Pete to his room and get him into dry clothes. I'll bag up a couple dozen cookies, and we'll head on over. Pete and I will go in the car, and since we don't have room for everyone, you kids can ride your bikes."

"Ah, Mom, not fair!" Kate almost wailed the words. "You'll get there first and find out what's happening before we do. We'll miss the big surprise."

Mom gave a soft huff. "Since Mrs. Maynard is your special friend, I guess it's only fair that I don't learn anything before the rest of you do. What if Pete and I stay in the car until you get there, or better yet, you take off first so you have a head start?"

Melissa released a loud breath. "Awesome. Thanks, Mrs. Ferris." She held out her hand to Pete. "Let's go get dressed so we can take a ride in the car, okay?" Suddenly, she fished in her pocket and pulled out the package of M&M's. "I brought these for you, and you can have them as soon as your clothes are changed."

Pete nodded and marched toward the back door into the house, his gaze fixed straight ahead. He came to an abrupt halt and turned. "Mouse and Rufus go for a ride with us?"

"Mrs. Maynard loves dogs and always says she wishes we'd bring Rufus, since she lost her pet. I don't see why we can't take them both in the car. But hurry up, Pete. Mrs. Maynard is waiting for us."

Thirty minutes later, all five kids rolled into the parking area next to Mrs. Maynard's garage and stopped by the Ferris family's Subaru. Kate's mom, Pete, Mouse, and Rufus all climbed out of the car while Kate and her friends parked their bikes. The front yard with its white picket fence erupted in gorgeous colors, with roses and daylilies vying for attention. Kate drew in a deep breath. "I love her flowers. Mom, we need to start something like this at our house."

Mom raised her brows. "Between caring for your brother, helping with the barn, fixing meals, doing housework, and shopping, I'm not sure I'd have a lot of time for gardening. But it is pretty." She cast a look around. "Mrs. Maynard said she'd be in the backyard with lemonade, so let's scoot on around there."

They walked the length of the house, Pete following his mother with head bowed, one hand on Rufus and the other on Mouse, and the rest of the group trooped along behind.

Kate's heartbeat revved up. She wondered if this mystery person was a relative of Mrs. Maynard who had come to visit, or maybe one of her old friends she'd known for years but rarely saw anymore. What would make her call and ask them all to come over? She guessed they'd find out soon enough. They rounded the corner, and Kate gasped, her hand flying to her mouth.

Mrs. Maynard sat in a lawn chair under a shade tree, sipping lemonade, and the man with the golden retriever sat in a chair beside her, holding her hand.

CHAPTER SIXTEEN

KATE STOPPED SO QUICKLY, TORI ran into her from behind. She couldn't believe what she was seeing. What was he doing here, and why was she allowing him to sit so close and hold her hand? This man must have found a way to deceive Mrs. Maynard or brainwash her somehow. He sat beside her, both of them in matching lawn chairs, with a blanket spread at their feet beneath a huge shade tree.

A low rumbling growl emanated from deep in Rufus's chest, and his hackles rose. Mouse wagged his tail and slobbered in the way only a Saint Bernard could do, and Kate looked from one to the other, then over at the retriever, the object of Rufus's unease. She lunged for her Rufus and grabbed his collar, but Pete knelt beside him with his hand on the big dog's head. He leaned close and whispered quiet words that Kate couldn't hear in Rufus's ear, then he stood, still patting the animal's head. Rufus instantly quieted beneath the little boy's touch, and Kate marveled again at how the dog responded to her brother.

Kate's mom looked from Kate to the man in the chair, who was holding his dog's leash. "Will your dog be all right? I can put Rufus in the car and open the windows. Or Martha, if you have a rope, I can tie him up in the shade, since the car would be awfully hot."

Pete shook his head. "Rufus is okay. Mouse is okay." He pointed at the retriever. "The new dog is okay." He turned to the owner but didn't raise his gaze as far as his face. "What's his name?"

"His name is Kenton, and my name is Barry. He's very gentle and won't hurt you."

Pete gave a brief nod. "He is my friend, too." He held out his hand, and the dog moved toward him, tail wagging. Pete stroked his silky head while the adults and kids watched. "Good boy," Pete crooned as he leaned close. "Rufus and Mouse are friends. Good boy." He sat down on the grass, and the retriever flopped down beside him, laying his head on Pete's leg. Mouse and Rufus sat on the other side, watching the new dog for a moment, then both of them lay down next to Pete and began to pant in the heat.

Martha rose from her lawn chair. "It doesn't appear we'll need to restrain Rufus or Kenton. Pete certainly has a way with animals, doesn't he, Nan?"

Kate's mother nodded and sat on the blanket on the other side of Rufus, keeping one hand on his collar. "Yes, he does, but I think I'll stay here anyway."

Mrs. Maynard smiled. "I see Melissa has the cookies. Thank you, dear." She extended her hand and took the bag Melissa offered. "Jake, Colt, Kate, it's so good to see you again." She reached out and gave Tori a hug. "How's my favorite horse owner? And how is Starlight today?"

"Great!" Tori hugged the older woman back. "We were getting ready to ride when you called."

"I'm sorry—I didn't mean to disrupt your day. Hopefully what I have to share will make it worthwhile." She went to a lawn table covered in a bright red-and-white cloth, where she had set a pitcher of iced lemonade and a tray of glasses. "I'll pour, and everyone can help themselves."

Kate took a glass and sank into a lawn chair, clutching her cold drink and staring at the man. He hadn't said another word. He looked harmless enough up close, Kate thought. His clothing was a little rumpled, but his hair was combed and his face and hands were clean, so maybe he wasn't a total bum. But why was he here, and what was he after? She glanced at

Colt, who also had his gaze trained on the man. They'd have to make sure he didn't pull a fast one on Mrs. Maynard.

The man pushed to his feet. "I'll go refill the lemonade pitcher. I'll be right back." He walked across the lawn toward the house.

Everyone settled into a chair or onto a blanket with their drinks and cookies, waiting for Mrs. Maynard to take her place and begin. She sipped her drink then released a long sigh. "I suppose I should begin. I know you must be wondering who this is and why he's here. You're probably also worried that I've allowed a stranger to come into my home, and that I'm not being careful about protecting myself."

Kate's mom quirked a brow. "I'll admit, the thought had crossed my mind. Is this the same man the kids saw in your woods? And the one who was asking questions about an older woman in the area by the name of Martha? If so, I'm concerned about the wisdom of inviting him here, unless you have a good reason."

Mrs. Maynard nodded, her face completely at peace. Her face was glowing when the man returned and set the pitcher on the table. "I couldn't agree more. But I think you'll agree with my reason when you hear it. This is Barry Jamison, my grandson."

"Oh!" Kate's mom said, her brows drawn together in a quizzical expression. Kate's breath released in a whoosh, and she heard Tori and Melissa both gasp. Colt gave a grunt that sounded suspicious, and Jake simply sat and stared. Pete continued to talk to the dogs while Mom looked from Barry to Mrs. Maynard and back.

Finally, Kate broke the silence. Someone had to protect the older woman from a scam artist. "But he's a stranger! He didn't even know your last name when he was asking about you." She shook her head. "There's no way he can be your grandson and not know your name."

Tori leaned forward in her chair. "And when we described him to you, you didn't seem like you knew who he was, either, Mrs. Maynard. Is it really safe to believe some stranger who comes in and claims to be your grandson?"

Colt thumped his fingers on the arm of his chair, all thought of chewing on a blade of grass forgotten. "Yeah. What does he want?" He swung his attention to the man. "What are you after? It was clear when we met you that you didn't know her at all, so this looks pretty fishy, if you ask me."

Jake cleared his throat. "This reminds me of that old Disney movie, *Candleshoe*, starring Jodie Foster. She's only a kid, but some hoodlums hire her to go to England and pretend to be the long-lost granddaughter of Helen Hayes. Jodie Foster was trying to find a hidden treasure in the mansion." He turned toward Mrs. Maynard. "You don't have a hidden treasure here, do you? Or something else this guy might want?"

Kate's mom choked back something that sounded like a cross between a laugh and a cry. "Kids! That's enough. I'm afraid we've all been rude to Mr. Jamison and Mrs. Maynard. We need to give them a chance to explain and not jump to conclusions when we don't know the facts." She looked from Kate to her friends, then over at Mrs. Maynard. "Although I'll confess I'm as confused and curious as the kids as to how this young man could be hunting for a woman who was his grandmother and not even know her name."

Mrs. Maynard clapped her hands together and laughed. "I was afraid you'd think something was amiss, but when I've explained, you'll understand. This is the first time I've met Barry. In fact, it's the first I even knew I had a grandson."

Jake's eyes rounded. "Shades of *Candleshoe*. I knew it. Treasure in the attic or buried in the back yard, I'll bet." He glared at Barry Jamison. "Are you a pirate in disguise or what? I could give you a whole list of pirate movies that deal with this kind of thing—"

Kate's mom reached over to where he sat on the other side of Mouse and touched his shoulder. "Maybe later, okay, Jake? We need to give Mrs. Maynard a chance to talk."

"Oh. Right." He pushed his glasses up his nose. "I did it again, huh. Talked too much. Motor-mouth, as my brother Jerry likes to call me. Never—"

"Hey, Jake." Colt held his finger up to his lips.

Jake drew a zipper across his closed mouth.

Mrs. Maynard chuckled. "You are a sweet boy, and I love hearing you talk, but yes, I'd like to explain. In fact, I think it might be better if you hear the story from Barry. He can explain it better than I can. Although I will tell you that his mother is my daughter, Martha Elizabeth."

Barry gave a slow nod. "Yes, her name was also Martha, after her mother."

Kate wrinkled her nose. "But if she's your grandmother, how could you go your whole life and never meet each other?"

Mrs. Maynard heaved a long, slow sigh, her expression sad. "My daughter and I had a huge disagreement many years ago, not long after she married. I was married to her father then, and widowed three years later. I got word to her that her father had died, and she attended his funeral, but she took care not to speak to me. I guess the hurt ran too deep."

Barry touched her arm in a comforting gesture. "My mother had a stubborn streak, but she lived to regret it. Unfortunately, that regret didn't show up until a couple of months ago. She'd never even told me I had a living grandmother. Anytime I'd asked questions about her family while growing up, she'd told me they were dead." He winced and shook his head. "I realize now she didn't want to be pestered to meet someone she'd cut out of her life, and she knew me well enough to know that when I got old enough, I probably would go looking on my own if I believed she was alive."

Kate's mom smiled. "But you said she came to regret her decision—and you're here—so what changed?"

Barry turned his head away, but not before Kate saw moisture brim in his eyes. "My mother died of cancer a couple of months ago." He turned back to face them. "A few days before she died, she told me she was sorry she'd never told me the truth. She gave me a picture of her and my grandmother together when they were both much younger, and explained that she'd grown up in the Hood River area, not far from here. But she said my grandmother didn't like living in town, and she might have moved farther into the country. So I started in Odell, hoping I might find a clue to her whereabouts."

Mrs. Maynard patted his hand. "It didn't help that I remarried twenty-five years ago and no one recognized the surname Barry's mother gave as her family name. If only I'd tried harder to make amends and keep in touch with Marty." She smiled. "That's what my husband called her, to keep from getting the two of us confused. All those wasted years . . ." Her eyes took on a faraway look and grew misty.

Kate had a hard time choking back the emotions that pushed to the surface. "Is it okay if we see the picture of you and your daughter that Barry brought?" Deep inside, she believed what Barry had shared was the truth, and that he wasn't trying to put something over on the older woman, but a part of her still wanted proof.

Mrs. Maynard gently reached into a pocket near the bottom edge of her oversized blouse. She withdrew a picture of a young woman standing next to an older woman who must have been Mrs. Maynard. "Here it is—this was taken many years ago. And here's one of Marty taken a year ago, with Barry and his father. Barry was twenty-six then." She handed the second photo to Kate.

She stared at the two women who must have been in their early twenties and late forties, if she was doing her math correctly. She could kind of see Mrs. Maynard in the older of the two, but she'd changed a lot in over thirty years. Then her gaze shifted to the photo of Barry with his parents, and she gasped. "Wow." She raised her head and met Barry's eyes. "Your mom looks like Mrs. Maynard did in this other photo. In fact, they could almost be sisters if you compare the two side-by-side."

Kate's mom held out her hand, and Kate passed them to her, sorry now that they'd questioned Barry's honesty. There was no doubt at all Barry was Mrs. Maynard's grandson.

As the photos were passed around, Kate couldn't help wondering something, but she wasn't sure if she should ask. Finally, she couldn't stand it any longer. "Excuse me, I know this is going to sound really weird, but—" She looked at Barry and almost bit back the words forming on her lips, knowing she'd regret them as soon as they were out. She drew in another breath and jumped in with both feet, feeling like maybe she'd switched places with Jake. "You haven't been letting horses loose as you've been wandering around the community, have you? And did you happen to drop a picture of a little kid with your dog while you were doing it?"

CHAPTER SEVENTEEN

KATE'S MOTHER GASPED AND STARED AT Kate. Tori and Melissa kept silent, but Jake let out a high-pitched squeak. Colt didn't say anything at all. Kate looked at him and saw him give such a slight nod that she wasn't sure was even a nod.

Then Colt reached into his hip pocket and pulled out the photo they'd found by the road. "I know Kate's question sounds pretty wild, but I have to admit the same thought crossed my mind." He shrugged. "Sorry, but we don't know anything about you, even if you are Mrs. Maynard's grandson. And the kid in this picture has similar coloring to you, only a lot younger—and the dog could be the same one you have now, or it's father or mother." He leaned over and handed Barry the photo.

The young man examined it closely, then looked up. "I can see why you'd think this could be Kenton, but the dog in the picture is smaller and his hair is a little shorter. He looks big because the boy is small, but he's not nearly as large or big boned as Kenton. Goldens often look similar, though, so I'm not surprised you'd think it might be the same dog." He handed the photo back to Colt. "And sorry, but I've never seen the boy before. He's wearing sneakers that were in style ten years ago, so it might be an old photo." He grinned. "And no, I haven't let any horses out, although you certainly don't have any reason to believe me."

Colt blew out a soft breath, and Kate groaned. She felt silly for saying anything, exactly like she knew she would. "Sorry. I shouldn't have asked about the horses without any proof. It's only—it all started happening at the same time you showed up—so we kind of thought . . ."

Barry held up his hand. "Hey, I get it. A stranger wandering the roads of a small community, asking questions, and walking with a dog that looks like one in a picture you found near a crime scene. I assume that's where you found it, right? I saw you kids looking in a ditch near a fence when I walked by not long ago. I wondered then what you were doing, but I didn't want to ask. I'd heard about the horses escaping—in fact, the sheriff stopped by my camp and questioned me pretty thoroughly—and I even wondered if the five of you might be the ones causing the trouble."

"Yikes!" Jake's voice cracked. "That's awful. Although I guess it's not much different than Robin Hood and his band of merry men being accused of all sorts of crimes by the Sheriff of Nottingham." He grinned. "Except we aren't grownups robbing the rich and giving to the poor, so maybe we should be Peter Pan and his band of lost boys—er—and girls." He slanted a look at the three girls sitting with their lips parted, shaking their heads at him. "That would be cool, huh, guys? We could have all kinds of adventures, even if people didn't understand."

Barry erupted in a shout of laughter. "You are too funny, kid. But seriously, I wasn't trying to accuse you of anything. Just telling you what I thought when I saw you searching the grass that day."

Colt poked Jake. "This is serious, Jake." He turned back to Barry Jamison. "So the sheriff talked to you and cleared you?"

"Colt!" Kate's mom's voice held a mild rebuke.

Barry held up his hand. "That's okay, it's a fair question, since I'm a stranger leading a dog like the picture you found. Yes, he cleared me. In fact, he's the reason I'm here today. I told him my grandmother's name from when she was married to my grandfather. He asked around, and a guy remembered both of them from years ago—and he knew Grandma remarried and settled in Odell. The sheriff checked me out to make sure I wasn't some kind of stalker, then he gave me her address and phone number. I called first before coming out and introducing myself and telling her my story."

Kate looked at Tori and Melissa, and their faces reflected the same discouragement she felt. She tried to straighten her spine and put on a brave front, but she wasn't feeling it inside. "It's really cool that you found each other. We love Mrs. Maynard, and it's great she discovered a grandson she didn't know she had. And we're glad one of our mysteries got solved, so now we know who you are and why you were asking about her—but I hate that we still don't know who let the horses out."

Kate rode her bike home with her friends, her mind still occupied with Mrs. Maynard's last comment—they shouldn't give up. If one mystery could be solved, the other one could be as well. "Hey, guys?"

Tori was the closest, and she looked over first. "Yeah? What's up?"

"I was thinking about what Mrs. Maynard said."

Melissa peddled up beside Kate. "About not giving up? You want to keep looking and see if we find anything else? We've done everything we know to do, and we found Rebel's owner. Maybe it's time to call it quits."

Tori braked to a stop, her eyes wide. The rest of her friends stared at her. Tori looked like she was struggling to form the words, and then pushed them out. "I can't believe that you, Melissa Tolbert, would give up. No way. That did not come out of your mouth. I'm the one who has to work through fear and wants to give up, not you or Kate. What's up with that?"

Melissa chuckled. "Sorry, Tori. I didn't mean to let you down. I guess I can't think of anything else we can do, is all. It's not that I'm afraid or want to quit. But it seems like we've hit a dead end."

Kate fiddled with a strand of hair that had loosened from her braid, wrapping one curl around her index finger. "Maybe, maybe not. I'm just saying we don't have any other clues, but I hate to give up. That's not like us. Know what I mean?"

They all nodded. Jake drew in a deep breath, his eyes sparkling, then he looked around at the others. "Not the right time for a movie analogy, right?"

"Right," all four of them echoed.

"We love you, Jake, truly we do," Kate said. "But how about putting that brilliant brain of yours to work on coming up with what we can do next. And the rest of us will pray. Maybe God has an answer." She grinned. "Race you all back to the barn!"

CHAPTER EIGHTEEN

THE FIVE OF THEM SLOWED TO a stop in front of the barn, and a sense of déjà vu took hold of Kate. Hadn't they lived through this entire scenario only a few days ago? Mom and Pete had driven home ahead of them, and both stood outside, silly grins on their faces, as Pete reached through the bars of the corral and stroked Rebel's face.

"You've got to be kidding me, Mom!" Kate said. "How did he get here again?"

Her mother stroked Pete's hair, and he was so engrossed with Rebel he didn't pull away or even flinch. "I have no idea. He was here when we drove in, patiently waiting like he'd been watching for us. He started prancing around as soon as Pete got out of the Subaru. I called Mrs. Marks, but no one was home, so I left her a message."

Kate pivoted with brows raised and stared at her friends. "Are you thinking what I'm thinking?"

Tori spoke up. "God brought an answer? You want to go to his pasture and see if someone let him out again? Maybe try to find a clue?"

"Right. Maybe we didn't look carefully enough the first time, who knows? There could be something we missed, or something new. Mrs. Marks gave us permission to search there before, right, Mom? Is it okay with you if we head over there? And if she comes home while we're there, we can let her know Rebel is here. I'd hate to take him back and find out the wire is cut or something."

"Yes, you have permission. I think it's a good idea. But please go straight there and back home again, and don't stop anywhere else. We've already had plenty of excitement for today, without anything else happening." She gave Pete a fond look. "Your brother and I will stay here and keep an eye on Rebel. I do kind of wish he hadn't come back, though. It's so hard on Pete when we take him home." She flicked her fingers toward their bikes. "You'd better go. The sooner you get over there and make sure the fence is fine, the sooner we'll be able to take care of our little problem."

Kate headed toward her bike with her friends following. What a crazy day! First they found out about Mrs. Maynard and her surprise grandson, then they came home to find Rebel here and now they were back on the hunt for clues to figure out how the horse escaped, in hopes it would lead to solving their final mystery.

"See you, Mom," she called over her shoulder. "We'll try to hurry. Hopefully we'll come home with a clue."

They pedaled as fast as they could, with Colt leading and Jake bringing up the rear, no one talking the entire way to the pasture where Rebel was supposed to reside.

Kate came to a halt at the gate and looked up the driveway toward the Marks's house. No sign of a car or any movement. "I guess we're on our own for now. But at least we'll see if anyone comes home while we're here. Mom left a message, so that's all we can do for now." She laid her bike over on the grass. "Let's spread out and check the entire front length of this fence along the road."

They moved down the fence about twenty paces apart, with Colt at the farthest distance and Jake near the driveway. Kate hated that the Marks family had used barbed wire to keep Rebel in. She shuddered, knowing what the spiked wire could do to a horse that got tangled up in it. She'd heard of one horse who pawed at a fence and sliced his fetlock joint right down to the muscle. The vet was able to sew him up, but he was lame for weeks. She was so thankful her grandpa had put up board fences topped with hot wire. No horses would get injured on their property.

She swung her attention back to the grass, kicking as she went. "Anyone having any luck yet?"

Tori was to her right and Melissa to her left. Both girls shook their heads but didn't reply, keeping their gazes trained on the ground.

Kate lifted her voice. "Hey, Jake. Anything?"

"Nope. Not even a rusty nail or a pop can. I can't believe how clean this ditch is. It's almost like someone came through here and cleaned it up." He straightened and stared. "Hey, do you think our perp did a sweep and removed all the evidence?"

Tori wrinkled her nose. "What's a perp? Sounds weird."

Jake jerked his head up and down. "Right. It's short for perpetrator, criminal, offender, culprit—"

Kate held up her hand. "Got it, thanks." She grinned. No one could say they didn't learn something new whenever Jake was around. "Hey, Colt, did you find anything over there? Jake says his area is clean. I haven't found much either, and neither has Tori or Melissa. Hopefully the 'perp' didn't do a thorough job in cleaning the entire ditch."

Colt didn't respond but reached out and touched the fence. "The wires have been cut."

All four of them raced along the ditch toward Colt, Jake arriving last. He puffed out a hard breath as he skidded to a halt. "The fence is cut? How can you tell? Maybe Rebel leaned against it, and it broke. Or maybe it rusted and snapped on its own." He pressed closer, adjusting his glasses and staring at the wire—the strands wrapped around the nearby wood post. "Nope." Colt pointed at the end of a wire. "For one thing, there's no way it would be neatly wrapped around the post. Someone hoped Rebel would jump out, but they didn't want him to get hurt by catching his legs in loose wire. Besides, if you look closely at the end of the wire, you can see there's no rust and it's shiny, like it was recently cut."

Melissa moved up beside Kate and pointed to the other side of the fence in the area where most of the grass had been grazed away. "You can see where Rebel's hooves dug in when he pushed off to jump. He must have noticed this low spot in the fence and decided to go visit Pete again. That horse sure has a thing for Pete." She grinned. "Of course, I get that, because I do, too. I can see why Rebel can't resist going back there. But this time he had help."

Kate heaved a sigh. "Now we have to figure out why. And the even bigger question—who's doing it."

Colt hadn't stopped his search along the base of the fence. He waved them over. "We haven't covered the entire area through here. I say we keep going all the way to the far corner. The person who did this might have been waiting till no one would see them cut the fence. They could have dropped something—especially if it was a kid with a backpack."

"Yeah," Jake said. "I don't know how many times I've forgotten to zip one of my compartments and lost a pen or notebook or part of my lunch. Mom's always telling me to be more careful, but sometimes I get in a hurry and I don't check the zipper. Want me to stay here while you guys fan out farther down the fence?" He gave them a hopeful look.

"You need more exercise, Jake," Kate said gently. "How about you going ahead? We'll follow and spread out. Jog on down to the corner, okay?" She gave him a mischievous smile, only half serious. If the younger boy objected, she'd be totally fine with him staying here.

"Take the lead?" He straightened and his narrow chest puffed out. "You mean like the lead detective on the case? Cool! You bet. And I won't let any clue go undetected. I'll make sure I track down anything that perpetrator left behind. No stone left unturned. No blade of grass unexamined, no—"

Colt gave him a nudge. "Sounds great, Jake. We know you can do it. It wouldn't surprise me if you're the one who finds the next clue."

Kate looked closely at Colt to see if he was teasing. Colt was usually the one who offered the most encouragement and support—or rather, he and Tori both did—but she didn't see even the tiniest bit of mischief or glint of teasing in his serious eyes.

"I have faith in you, too, Jake. If anyone can figure out a clue, it's you. Honestly, you're one of the smartest kids I know." And she meant it. Jake really was smart. He had an odd way of showing it sometimes, but the kid had brains.

Jake set off down the fence line with determined strides. Colt followed, then Kate, Melissa, and Tori covered the area closest to the cut fence. All five of them kept their gazes roving from the road to the fence and the entire area in between, as silence covered the group. Several minutes ticked by, and Kate was about ready to call a halt and suggest they head home, when a shout brought her head up.

Jake waved his arms in the air and jumped up and down, nearly sending his glasses flying. Excitement seemed to burst from every part of his body. "I found something!" he hollered. He held up a small book. "It's a library book. If it belongs to the person who cut the fence, we can track him down by returning the book to the library and asking who checked it out!"

CHAPTER NINETEEN

KATE AND HER FRIENDS SAILED INTO the barnyard, their chests heaving from their fast ride. Jake had the book tucked under his belt, refusing to turn it over to anyone else's care. It was obvious he was proud of having been the one to find it. Kate hoped they could discover who checked out the book and confront them. Would a librarian give out that information? She had no idea. It would probably be better if Mom or Dad talked to someone there. She doubted the librarians would tell a kid anything that might be considered confidential.

"Hey, Mom!" Kate was thrilled to see Pete and her mother still outside petting Rebel. Maybe Mrs. Marks had returned right after they left her place, and she was on her way here to talk about what to do. She'd have to get that fence fixed before she could put Rebel back in the pasture. She was kind of getting used to having that horse around. It wouldn't hurt her feelings if her little brother got to spend a bit more time with his new friend.

Her mother looked over at them. "Did you find anything? You took a little longer than I expected. I hope that means you have good news."

Jake pulled the book out of its place behind his belt and waved it in the air. "We found another clue."

Tori stopped her bike next to his. "He means *he* found another clue. He's a great detective."

"Thanks!" Jake's grin widened. "But I guess we kind of have good news and bad."

Colt leaned his bike against a tree. "Yep. The top strand of the fence was cut, clean as anything, and the wire was wrapped around a fence post. Somebody did this on purpose. Sure wish we could catch them in the act. It makes me mad they'd endanger a horse that way."

Jake tipped his head to the side. "Endanger? They cut the wire and moved it so he wouldn't get hurt. Rebel doesn't have any cuts on his legs, does he?" He walked toward the corral and looked through the bars.

Melissa gave a grunt that sounded like irritation. "That's not the point, Jake. I know you're not a horse person, and obviously whoever cut the fence isn't either. What if Rebel wasn't a good jumper? What if he tried to clear it and caught his hooves on the second wire? He could have landed on his knees on the gravel road, or gotten badly cut, or tangled his leg in that wire." She shuddered. "I hate to even think of the damage he could have done. It was stupid and irresponsible, and someone needs to get in big trouble for this."

Kate bit her lip. "I've been having a hard time with being super angry at whoever's been doing this. I want them to pay for what they've done. I mean, I know we're supposed to forgive, but I don't want to. It's not right to put so many horses in danger and to scare their owners, and have people's property torn up by loose horses grazing in their yards."

Nan's face grew serious. "I agree, it's not right or fair. And yes, it makes me mad, too. There's nothing wrong with being angry. Even Jesus got mad when he drove the money changers out of the temple. But it's what we do with it that matters. The Bible says not to let the sun go down on our anger. That usually means we're supposed to go to the person we're mad at and try to make it right or resolve the problem if we can. That's not possible, since we don't know who we're mad at. So what should we do in that case?"

Kate looked down at the ground and scuffed her toe in the gravel, not liking where this was leading. She wanted to stay angry. She had a right to be mad at whoever was doing this, didn't she? Maybe she'd wait and see what some of the other kids said before she blurted out something that would make her look stupid or uncaring.

"I can't stop thinking about what it would be like if somebody let Starlight loose and he got hit by a car, or tangled in wire, or got lost and never returned." Tori's soft voice broke the silence—Tori, the one who was always so kind and forgiving. "I'm sorry, Mrs. Ferris, but I am mad. Furious. I have been since this started."

Something inside Kate broke. She felt shocked that her kindhearted friend would feel this way. Kate was the one who usually had trouble letting go of things—not Tori or Colt. Both of them were so laid back and nice. At one time she would have expected Melissa to respond like this, but Tori? She couldn't believe it.

"I'm not a horse person," Jake said, "so it probably doesn't hit me as hard as all of you guys who own a horse, but I've seen how Pete loves Rebel. When I saw that cut wire, then Melissa explained what could have happened, it made me sick to my stomach. It is hard to forgive someone who'd pull a dirty trick like that."

Colt hadn't said a word through the entire discussion, but now he cleared his throat. "I'll take a stab at answering your questions, Mrs. Ferris. But it doesn't come from me. It comes from a devotion my dad read to our family the other night. I didn't totally get it at the time, but it's making a lot more sense now."

Kate's mom leaned her shoulder against a rail of the corral. She glanced once at Pete, who continued to pet Rebel and croon soft words to the horse, then she returned her attention to Colt. "I'd love to hear what your dad shared and how you think it applies to all of this, Colt."

"It's nothing really huge, but I think I get it now. He said that forgiving someone doesn't mean we agree with what they did. We forgive other people when they hurt us, so we can keep from getting bitter and hard inside."

Jake gaped at Colt. "Huh? I don't get it."

"I didn't either, but I think I do now. If we choose to forgive the guy who's doing this stuff, it doesn't mean it's okay that he's been turning horses loose. And like Mrs. Ferris said, it's okay to be mad at him for doing it. But if we hold onto that anger, then we start getting ugly inside—it festers and builds poison inside our souls like a zit. If we forgive that person, then Dad says we're not holding them hostage, plus God can clean up and heal our hearts. I don't get how all of that works, but I did understand the part about not saying what they did was okay just because we forgive. That makes sense to me."

Mrs. Ferris touched Colt's shoulder. "You're right—and we don't have to understand it all. I think the point is, we can choose to stay angry, or we can choose to forgive and let God deal with the person's wrong choices. We can't make anyone else change. Only God can do that. So if we let go of it all, He's free to try to change that person. It's still their choice, but we don't get in the way with our anger. It's a good lesson for all of us."

Kate bit her lip. "Okay, I guess. It's not easy to do that, though. And does that mean the person who's doing all this gets off without consequences?"

"No way!" Melissa spoke before anyone else could. "It better not mean that."

Kate's mom shook her head. "No. Absolutely not. They still need to pay for their actions. It'll be up to the sheriff and the courts what happens to them, not us."

"So you're saying even if they get arrested, we still need to forgive them? It sounds weird to me."

Her mother smiled. "Remember, hon, God forgave all of us. We're not perfect. We've all sinned, right? So we shouldn't do any less."

"Okay, I guess that makes sense. It's not easy, though. Not after all the harm that could have been done. It's a miracle no horses got hurt." Kate winced at the thought of what could have happened.

"Yes," Mom agreed, "a miracle. So let's concentrate on that and let God take care of whoever did this. That's His job, not ours."

CHAPTER TWENTY

KATE'S PARENTS STILL HADN'T HEARD FROM Mrs. Marks by the next day, so Nan Ferris decided to drive over. She planned to stop by the library on the way and see if the librarian would give her any information about the book's borrower. There was a possibility it was only lost, so she decided not to turn it over to the sheriff until she learned more.

Kate and her friends stayed outside with Pete, who spent every possible minute with Rebel, feeding his friend carrots. Kate's mom had gone into the corral before she left that morning, and the horse had allowed her to brush him and untangle his mane, as long as Pete was standing nearby. Kate still couldn't believe the effect her brother had on the big gelding. Maybe they'd have to call him Angel instead of Rebel after all. She giggled.

"What's funny?" Jake peered at her through his thick lens. "I didn't hear anyone tell a joke. Did I miss something?"

"I don't think you missed anything," Melissa said, "but I'm kind of curious too. Sure doesn't seem like there's been much happening lately worth laughing over."

"But lots of funny stuff, huh?" Jake bobbed his head. "Get it? Not funny ha-ha, but funny stuff. A play on words, you know?"

Tori elbowed him. "Good one, Jake. What's up with you, Kate?"

"It's not a big deal. I was only thinking that maybe we were wrong and we should have named him Angel, after all." She pointed at the big horse, who stood with his head drooping as Pete scratched under his forelock. "The big baby. And to think I was terrified of him when he first got here."

Colt shifted the straw between his lips to the other side of his mouth. "He needed the right touch, that's all. I think he's found a best friend with Pete."

"Yeah," Tori said, "and vice versa."

"How much longer till your mom gets back, Kate?" Jake squirmed in the lawn chair he'd pulled under the shade of a big tree near the corral. "I'm about to burst, I'm so excited to see if the librarian tells her anything. And I'm sure glad for this shade."

The sound of tires on gravel alerted them to a car pulling into the area near the barn. A car door slammed, and Kate's mom walked around the corner of the barn toward them. She didn't even have a chance to speak before Kate and her friends rushed her.

Nan held up her hands. "Hey, there! Hold it—don't knock me over. Give me a chance to catch my breath."

Anxiety beat through Kate's heart. She knew she needed to get better at trusting God, but this was so important. She stilled herself and whispered, "Sorry, Lord," then touched her mother's arm. "Did you get any information?"

Nan nodded and sank into the chair Jake had vacated. "Whew. Sure glad the car has A/C. It's hot out here. This shade is nice, though."

"Mrs. Ferris!" Melissa said, and Tori groaned.

She looked at them, then over at Pete, who was engrossed in his own world. "He's been good while I've been gone?"

Kate wanted nothing more than to get an answer to their question, but knowing her mother would take care of the most important thing first before moving on. "Yes, Mom. Rebel is the perfect babysitter."

Pete swung around and looked toward Kate. "I am not a baby." Then he pivoted toward the horse and resumed stroking its face.

Kate gaped at her mother, who blew out a soft breath. "Wow."

Kate nodded. "Double wow. That's not like Pete, but it's pretty cool. Okay, Mom, spill. You're killing us!"

She chuckled and shifted her weight in the chair. "Thankfully, a librarian I've known for years was on duty when I got there. I explained what had been happening and that I didn't want to turn the book over to the sheriff, but I might need to. I told her if it was checked out by a young person we know, it might be better if your dad and I have a chance to talk to them first, in case it's nothing connected with our case."

Colt sank onto the grass near her feet. "Smart thinking. What did she say?"

"She agreed that was sound reasoning. But frankly, I'm not sure what to think about what I found out. It could mean a lot, or nothing at all."

Kate slapped the palm of her hand against her forehead. "Mom!"

"Right. Sorry. I apologize, as Jake would say." She shot him a grin then quickly sobered. "The book was checked out by Kyle Marks."

Colt's low whistle was the only sound that followed.

Kate opened her mouth to reply, but the sound of another car pulling into the parking area on the other side of the barn stopped her. "We must have boarders coming to ride, but it's awfully hot. Nobody comes in the middle of the day during the summer."

Her mother got to her feet. "Let's table this discussion until we see who's here. I'll walk over and see who it is. We don't want anyone else involved, especially if Kyle simply dropped the book on his way home."

Kate crinkled her brow. "Not likely, Mom. It was way at the end of the fence, in an area of trampled grass. It looked like someone had been waiting down in that ditch for a while. And it wasn't that far from where the fence was cut. But why in the world would Kyle do something like that?"

"Like what?" Mrs. Marks stepped around the corner of the barn toward them.

Kate winced, realizing she'd forgotten to lower her voice. "Sorry, Mom," she whispered, knowing it was too late for an apology.

Her mother barely gave a nod, keeping her eyes fixed on Mrs. Marks. "Hello, Gloria. You must have gotten my message about Rebel."

Another car door slammed, and Kyle appeared around the corner of the barn.

Mrs. Marks marched up and stopped close to Kate's mom. "I'd like to know what your daughter meant by her remark about my son."

Kate wanted to groan and hide her face in her hands. She'd really blown it now. She glanced at her friends and saw various degrees of surprise and concern clouding their expressions. They weren't sure what to expect, either. She hoped God would give her some of that wisdom her dad liked to talk about.

Before her mom could reply, another car pulled into the parking area. A minute later, Barry Jamison came around the corner, accompanied by Mrs. Maynard. The older woman smiled and waved, and Barry nodded to Kate's mom. "I'm sorry, I hope we're not interrupting. I wanted to say goodbye before I head home and thank you for all you've done for my grandmother—and to tell you the good news."

Kate's mother motioned for him to join them. "I hope you won't mind, Gloria—and you might prefer not to talk about our business in front of anyone else—Barry is on his way back home, if you'd give us a minute?" She turned to Barry. "We'd love to hear good news. What's up?"

"Since my mother passed away, I have no reason to return to Northern California. I'll go pack up the things I want to keep and get the house on the market, but then I'm coming back here to stay with Grandma." He looped an arm around her shoulders and gave her a gentle squeeze. "She's in excellent health now, but we're both lonely, and I want to be here to help care for the place."

Murmurs of excitement and approval went through the group. Mrs. Maynard beamed, but Kate noticed Gloria frowning and Kyle edging toward the car. She'd almost forgotten the pair. Hopefully her mom would talk to them soon. It probably wasn't nice that they'd been ignored ever since Barry and Mrs. Maynard arrived.

But Kate was thrilled about Barry's news—Mrs. Maynard did get lonely, and they weren't able to visit often enough to help with all the little chores that needed to be done around her property.

Barry's big golden retriever tugged at his leash, and Pete dropped to one knee and held out his arms. The dog dashed over, wiggling like he'd found a new friend. "Good boy, Kenton."

Kate's mom raised her brows at Barry. "I hope you don't mind. As you may remember from when we met at your grandmother's house, my son is a bit of an animal whisperer."

"So is my dad." Kyle stepped forward, his gaze fixed on the dog. "He had a dog that looked like that. His name was Corey. He was supposed to be my dog. We got him when I was little, but he took to my dad and barely paid attention to me, even though I loved him. I have a picture of me when I was little with Corey. It's all I have left of him, since Dad took him away when he deserted us." He pulled out his wallet and flipped through it. Then Kate saw the boy's eyes cloud over. Something like anger tugged at his mouth, and his head jerked up. "Mom! Did you do anything with my picture? It's not here!" True panic filled his face.

Colt stuck his hand into his shirt pocket. "Would this happen to be it?" He handed the photo they'd found to Kyle.

Relief bowed Kyle's shoulders, and tears filled his eyes. "Yeah. Thanks. Where'd you find it?" He glanced at Colt then around the silent group.

Colt fished in his other pocket. "How about this? Did you lose it at the same time?" He dug out the silver band with the initials.

Awareness jolted through Kate. K-M. Kyle Marks. She wanted to slap her forehead. Why hadn't she thought of him? Because he was new to the area and his family's horse had been one of the first to escape, that was why. But it didn't make a bit of sense.

He stretched out his hand, and the color drained from his face. "Where... where..."

His mother looked from one to the other, then at the items her son held. "Kyle, that bracelet belonged to your father. Why do you have it? I assumed he took it with him." She raised her brows at Kate's mom. "They have the same initials."

Kyle turned on her, anger blazing from his eyes. "It was supposed to be mine. Like Corey was supposed to be mine. Like Dad's love was supposed to be mine. But did he care? No. He threw me away. That's why I—" The rest of the color drained from his face, and his head drooped.

His mother touched Kyle on the shoulder. "Why you what, son?"

He didn't answer but simply stood there, unmoving.

Kate's mom softly cleared her throat. "Gloria, the kids found the top strand of fence at your place cut. Someone was careful enough to wrap the loose wire around the post so Rebel wouldn't get tangled in it, but it's obvious the person wanted him to escape. And what Kate meant was, why would Kyle, or anyone, want to do that?" Before Mrs. Marks could respond, Nan interjected. "The kids found a library book on the ground not far from where the wire was cut, and a librarian said it was checked out to Kyle."

Mrs. Marks seemed to stagger, and Barry Jamison steadied her and guided her to a lawn chair in the shade. "I don't know for sure what's going on, but you need to sit before you fall." He turned his attention to Kyle. "Young man, it sounds as though you might have some explaining to do."

Kyle started to tremble, then he bolted and ran, heading toward the road.

Barry put his fingers to his lips and gave a high-pitched whistle. "Retrieve, boy." His dog took off after Kyle, tail wagging like it was some kind of game.

Mrs. Marks gasped. "Is he going to bite my son?"

"No, ma'am. He'll tackle him and hold him until I get there, but mostly he'll just sit on Kyle. He won't bite unless I tell him to, so don't worry." Barry jogged toward the boy, who now lay on the ground with the big dog standing over him, alternately growling softly and then licking the boy's face as if in apology. Barry called off his dog and pulled Kyle to his feet.

Mrs. Marks ran to her son and wrapped her arms around him. "Are you hurt?"

He shook his head but didn't reply.

She grabbed his shoulders and stood nose-to-nose with him. "Why did you run? I need to know what's going on with you, Kyle. You haven't been the same since—" She sucked in a breath and stopped.

He glared at her, shaking her hands loose. "Since Dad left, you mean? What did you expect? He takes my dog with him, I have to steal the silver bracelet he promised me after I found it packed in his suitcase, and he didn't even say goodbye. I can't believe he didn't take his precious horse with him, too.

He always loved that horse more than he loved me. That's why I hate Stupid so much, or whatever his name is." He took a step away. "So much that I wanted him gone, and I did whatever it took to make sure that happened."

Chapter TWENTY-ONE

KATE, HER PARENTS, AND HER FOUR FRIENDS all sat in lawn chairs in Kate's backyard on a warm, late-summer afternoon. A very patient Rufus and Mouse allowed Pete to splash water on them from his wading pool, while the rest of the group drank iced tea and lemonade in the shade of an old oak.

Kate set her glass down on a small table. "I feel bad that we had to call the sheriff and turn Kyle in. I wish we could have done what we did when we found Mom's money box, instead of getting the police involved."

Kate's dad shifted in his chair. "But do you understand why we wouldn't do that? Do you realize the difference?"

Jake waved his hand in the air. "Can I take a stab at that, sir?"

John Ferris grinned. "Sure, Jake."

"When the box was stolen and then returned, all the money was there, no one was hurt, and it was only your property that was taken. You were willing to pay the money back to the fund if you had to. So nothing was done to anyone else, and you could choose whether to press charges or not. Is that right?"

"Yes, it is. And I'm impressed you figured that out."

Jake straightened his shoulders. "I'm going to be a detective someday. Besides, it makes sense. But I'm not completely sure why we couldn't all forgive Kyle since no horses were hurt."

Colt leaned forward. "I think I know. The sheriff was already involved in this case, and horses could have been hurt. It wasn't only his horse that he let out. If it had been, then it would be up to his mom to decide his punishment. But what he did affected close to a dozen people, and that's pretty serious."

Tori looked as though she might cry. "I hope they won't put him in jail."

"Yeah, I get where he's coming from," Melissa said. "My dad took off and left my mom and me, too. It's hard not to be resentful and want to try to get even. I know it doesn't make a lot of sense what he did, but I think I understand what made him do it."

Tori scrunched her forehead. "But why let the other horses out? Why not only Rebel if that's the horse he hated?"

"He figured if he turned a lot of horses loose, no one would suspect him." Kate shrugged. "Or at least, that's what it seems like."

The group was silent, and Kate's heart hurt for Melissa, as well as for Kyle. Her friend had been through so much of her own grief this summer, and it had to cut deep seeing how upset Kyle was over the loss of his dad. "Do you think they'll send him to jail, Dad?"

Her dad gave a half-smile. "I know they won't. I spoke to the sheriff. He's recommending leniency to the judge, based on what Kyle's already gone through. But he's going to have to do around a hundred hours of community service the rest of the summer and on weekends, all the way until Christmas. And the sheriff is talking to his mom about getting Kyle involved in the local Big Brother program that started recently. I'd suggest you kids try to be his friend, but I think he'll need space first to work through his anger and embarrassment. I'm guessing someone a little older might be a better mentor for now. But keep your eyes open in the future. You never know how you might be able to help, since all of you except Colt attend the same school."

Kate drummed her fingers on the arm of her lawn chair. "Now the other big question. In all the excitement, Mrs. Marks didn't say when she's going to get the fence fixed and have us take Rebel home."

Pete's head rose, and he stared straight at Kate. "Not take Rebel home. Keep Rebel here. Rebel is my friend."

A huge smile broke out on their mom's face. Kate knew it had to be because Pete had actually made eye contact with someone, and her heart warmed at that fact. "Actually," Kate's mom said, "we aren't going to take Rebel home, Pete."

Everyone in the circle gasped, and Kate's friends pummeled her mom with questions. Then a hush settled over the yard when Pete stood in the little pool, water dripping from his small body. "Rebel will stay here. This is Rebel's home." He moved his gaze from Kate to his mother before dropping down into the pool again, humming his favorite song.

"Mom?" Kate's voice broke exactly like Jake's had not long ago. "What's going on?"

Her mother shot a look at her dad, and he smiled. "Want me to tell them?"

"Yep."

"Mrs. Marks doesn't want Rebel back. She said it's too hard for Kyle to be around him. She also thinks Rebel belongs with Pete. No one in their family could handle the horse other than her husband, and it's obvious he doesn't want him. He left the papers there, and she's going to sign him over to our family." He laughed. "I think Rebel has proven he's not such a rebel after all, and he's found a new home. I'm not so sure we need another horse, but it's apparent it's important to Pete, and that's important to your mom and me. So, Rebel now belongs to your brother."

The entire group sat stunned for several seconds, then Jake jumped to his feet, his fist punching into the air. "All right! Way to go, Pete! Hurrah! Bravo! Congrats!"

Pete looked up and smiled, then slowly he rose to his feet again. He did a tiny dance in place in the water, stomping his feet and splashing around, before sitting back down like nothing had happened.

Colt reached up and pulled Jake back into his chair. "Yep, and we all agree with you, Jake. And besides that, God is good." He shot a glance at Pete and grinned.

"All the time." Kate echoed the refrain after him, a satisfied smile tugging at her lips. She wanted to dance and shout for joy herself. How could she ever have doubted the fact that God loved them and cared what happened in their lives?

Hopefully, when the next hard thing hit, she would think back to today and remember God's amazing answers to her prayers. In fact, maybe she needed to start keeping a journal

of answered prayers along with her thoughts and memories —
and the struggles she had to work through. It might even help
her not to stumble and fall the next time she was tempted to
get angry, be unforgiving, or forget to trust God.

Kate looked around the circle at the happy faces of her
family and friends, and thanked God once again for the
wonderful blessings He had poured out in her life.

AUTHOR'S NOTE

I've been an avid horse lover all of my life. I can't remember a time when I wasn't fascinated with the idea of owning a horse, although it didn't happen until after I married. While growing up, I lived in a small town on a couple of acres that were mostly steep hillside—other than our lawn and garden area, there was no room for a horse. I lived out my dreams by reading every book I could find that had anything to do with horses.

My first horse was a two-year-old Arabian gelding named Nicky, who caused me to fall deeply in love with the Arabian breed. Over the years we've owned a stallion, a number of mares, a handful of foals, and a couple of geldings. It didn't take too many years to discover I couldn't make money in breeding. After losing a mare and baby due to a reaction to penicillin, and having another mare reject her baby at birth, we decided it was time to leave that part of the horse industry and simply enjoy owning a riding horse or two.

Our daughter, Marnee, brought loving horses to a whole new level. She was begging to ride when she was two to three years old, and riding her own pony alone at age five. Within a few years, she requested lessons, as she wanted to switch from

Western trail riding to showing English, both in flat work and hunt-seat, and later, basic dressage. I learned so much listening to her instructor and watching that I decided to take lessons myself.

We spent a couple of years in the show world, but Marnee soon discovered she wanted to learn for the sake of improving her own skills more than competing, and she became a first-rate horsewoman.

We still ride together, as she and her husband, Brian, own property next to ours. My old Arabian mare, Khaila, was my faithful trail horse for over seventeen years and lived with Marnee's horses on their property, so she wouldn't be lonely. At the age of twenty-six, she began having serious age-related problems and went on to horse heaven in late July of 2013. I ride Brian's Arabian mare, Sagar, now, when Marnee and I trail ride. I am blessed to have a daughter who shares the same love as I do and to have had many wonderful years exploring the countryside with my faithful horse Khaila.

If you don't own your own horse yet, don't despair. It might not happen while you still live at home, and you might have to live out your dreams in books, or even taking a lesson at a local barn, but that's okay. God knows your desire and will help fulfill it in His perfect way.

SECRETS FOR YOUR DIARY

Secret #1

Have you ever done something that turned out to be dangerous, even though it seemed safe at the time? Kate goes in the corral with a strange horse and snaps a rope on its halter, assuming the horse is tame. He rears, giving Kate a bad scare. How do Kate's parents react to her decision to approach a horse she doesn't know? What should have been the consequences for Kate's poor decision? Put yourself in Kate's place, and imagine instead the strange animal is a dog you don't know that is running loose. What decision would you make, and why? What might be the outcome of your decision?

Note from Kate

I should have reacted differently, but I was so sure Rebel would be tame, like all of our horses are, that I didn't think about him being wild. As soon as he pulled back and reared, I realized I'd made a bad decision. My parents were right to be upset. I could have been seriously hurt. Next time something like that happens, I'll talk to my parents first, before I try to do it on my own.

Secret #2

Do you have a friend who is different from other kids and sometimes gets teased because of it? Or maybe you're the different one who doesn't quite fit in? Kate and her friends accept Jake into their group, even though Kate says talking to him is like walking into a whirlwind. He isn't anything like her other friends, and sometimes dealing with his quirky personality takes a lot of patience. Can you think of anyone at your school or church who seems odd or strange, but maybe is just lonely? What would it take for you to approach that person and be a friend to him or her? What do you think would happen if you tried?

Note from Kate

I wasn't too sure about Jake when I first met him—he was kind of weird, but funny, too. It didn't take long for him to win me over. Jake is fun to joke around with, but I know teasing can turn mean if we aren't careful. Jake doesn't deserve that—he's a cool guy, and just like I learned with Melissa, I need to be careful not to judge too harshly until I understand the situation.

Secret #3

Have you prayed and prayed for something that still hasn't happened? Kate has been praying for her little brother, Pete, for years. She hopes that camp will make a change in his behavior. Kate wants Pete to be a normal, pesky little brother who runs and plays and talks like all the other little kids. What are some reasons God might not be answering Kate's prayer right away? If God says "No," or is silent, is that an answer to prayer too, just like when He says "Yes"? How long should Kate keep praying for her brother?

Note from Kate

I guess it's bothered me for a long time that God hasn't healed Pete. But then I see the amazing way he connects with animals and what a special kid he is, and I know God doesn't make mistakes. Now, I try to trust God with my little brother. We're seeing changes, a little at a time, so I'm going to keep on praying and believing that something extra special will happen in the future. I've decided to be happy with the little changes we see in Pete. It's so exciting to see even a small improvement!

Secret #4

Can you think of a time when you were punished for something you did? How did you feel about being caught? Was it more painful to be punished or to be found out? Kate feels bad for Kyle, who acted out after his dad left the family. Kate doesn't want to turn him in to the sheriff, although her parents say it's the right thing to do. What do you think should have happened to Kyle? What lessons should Kyle learn from his punishment of community service?

Note from Kate
It was really hard for me when horses kept being turned loose—they could have been hurt, or hurt someone else. I didn't want to get so angry that my anger turned to hate. Mom and Dad told me that hate does more harm to the person who hates than the one we're mad at. When I discovered it was Kyle, and how hurt he was over his dad leaving his family, I understood that we don't see all the reasons a person acts the way they do. Now I'm going to pray for Kyle, that God will heal his heart.

JAKE'S FAVORITE COOKIES

Here is Jake's favorite, easy recipe for Apple Raisin Walnut Cookies.

Ingredients:
1 cup raisins	2 to 2 1/4 cups flour
1/2 cup shortening	1 tsp baking powder
1 1/3 cups brown sugar	1 tsp cinnamon
1 large egg	3/8 tsp cloves
1/4 cup milk	1/2 tsp salt
1 cup chopped apples	1/2 tsp nutmeg
	1 cup chopped walnuts

In saucepan, cover raisins with water, bring to a boil, remove from heat and let stand for 5 minutes. Drain.
In large bowl cream shortening and sugar. Add egg and milk.
Mix dry ingredients and add.
Beat till blended.
Add nuts, apple, and raisins.
Drop on ungreased baking sheet.
Bake at 375 degrees 8–10 minutes or until done.
Best stored in airtight container.

Now, a Sneak Peek at Book Two—
Trouble on the Trail
Releasing Spring of 2017

Chapter One

Kate bounced on her toes, so excited she could hardly stand it. "Can you believe we're going to get to go on a trail ride up in the Mount Hood wilderness area, Tori? It doesn't get much better than that!"

Tori stopped grooming Starlight long enough to swipe a strand of dark hair out of her eyes. "Yeah, pretty cool. Do Melissa and Colt know? Are they coming along? And how about Jake? He doesn't ride anything but his bike."

Kate felt like a balloon that landed on a sharp object as her joy evaporated. "Bummer. I didn't even think about Jake. I wish he'd learn to ride. I hate that he gets left out of fun stuff like a trail ride." She slipped Capri's fly mask onto her face then tightened the Velcro strap under her chin. "But Colt and Melissa are both going to come. At least, I sure hope so! I can't imagine not having all of us there."

"Your parents are going, right?" Tori unsnapped the lead rope from the ring mounted in the alleyway then pulled

Starlight around toward the outer door. "We're putting them out in the pasture, right?"

"Yep. It's late enough in the summer that we don't have to worry about them foundering now. It's nice for them not to be cooped up in a stall or a dry paddock. They love grazing even if the grass isn't very green."

They watched Capri and Starlight trot a few strides across the pasture before settling down to graze.

Gravel sprayed their legs and they turned. Colt sat on his bike next to Jake, both of their freckled faces stretched in wide smiles. Jake adjusted his glasses. "What's up, girls? You just get done riding?" He looked from the barn to the house and back to Kate and Tori. "Where's Melissa?"

Tori shrugged. "She was supposed to be here, but we finished our ride and she hasn't shown up. Not sure what's going on."

Jake grinned. "I snagged my brother's phone. He left it on the dining table when he went to work this morning, so I figured, why let it go to waste? Want me to call her?"

Colt whistled. "Man, Jerry will nail you if he finds out you have it. Not sure that's smart, Jake."

"How's he gonna know? I'll get home before he does and put it back."

"Uh, Jake." Colt waved his hand in front of Jake's face. "What if he sees Melissa's number on his phone as the last person called? He's going to know he didn't call her, right? So you'll be toast when he finds out you did."

"Oh. Right." Jake bit his lip then tucked the phone back into his pocket. "Guess I'd better not call."

All of them turned as a car pulled into the barn parking lot. A door slammed and Melissa jogged toward them, waving at her mother as the car backed toward the gravel road. "Hey, guys." She came to a stop a few feet from the boys on their bikes. "Sorry I'm late. Mom wanted me to help her put groceries away after she went shopping, then I had to do the dishes. I thought we'd never get done. Now she's on her way to see a friend, so I'm free for a couple of hours. What's up?"

Kate shot a look at Jake. "Well, uh . . . Tori and I were talking about a trail ride up at the base of Mount Hood in a couple of weeks. It's our last big ride before school starts. Mom and Dad said all of you can come if you want to camp out one night and bring your horses."

"Cool!" Colt pumped his fist. "Sounds like a perfect end to the summer."

Jake kicked at a rock. "Yeah. Perfect. For people who ride horses."

"Oh man, I wasn't thinking." Colt's face fell. "I'm sorry."

Melissa bumped Jake's arm with her elbow. "Hey, I know! We have two weeks. How about you take riding lessons on Kate's lesson horse, Mr. Gray? You could go with us that way."

Tori clapped her hands. "That would be awesome, Jake! You have to come. You just have to!"

Kate looked from one to the other and nodded. "That would work, if you're willing, Jake. What do you think?"

Jake looked like he'd been slammed in the stomach by a kickball. "Uh. No. Nada. Negatory. Not gonna happen. You aren't getting me on one of those monsters." He backed away from the pasture where Capri and Starlight grazed. "It's my bike all the way. I'll go camping and take my bike, but I'm not going to bet killed by one of those beasts. But I came to tell you something else. I didn't even tell Colt on the way over, and I'm about to bust." He pushed his glasses up again, looking at the other kids through his lenses with wide eyes and his lips pressed together.

"So, give!" Kate laughed.

"Yeah, Jake. You were about to bust, and now you're holding out." Melissa shook her head.

"Fine. No problemo. Gotcha. I just heard about another mystery happening in the area, and I think we need to figure it out."

ACKNOWLEDGMENTS

This series has been a brand-new adventure for me—one I never expected, but one I'm so blessed to have experienced. I've loved horses all my life and owned them since I was 19, but never thought I'd write horse novels for girls. I'm so glad I was wrong!

So many people have helped make this series possible: My friends at church, who were excited when I shared God's prompting and offered to pray that the project would find a home. My family, my friends, and my critique group, who believed in me, listened, read my work, and cheered me on. There have also been a number of authors who helped me brainstorm ideas for the series or specific sections of one book or the other when I struggled—Kimberly, Vickie, Margaret, Cheryl, Lissa, Nancy—you've all been such a blessing!

And special thanks to my sister, Jenny Mertes, for her expert job on editing this book. You rock, sis!

But there's a special group of kids I especially want to thank. Two different times I posted on Facebook, asking my readers if they had ideas and could give me honest feedback. A number of people responded not only on the plot, but gave me feedback on the cover. I love my readers!

I'm so thrilled I got to meet my graphic artist, Kirk DouPonce, and the models for my books. It was such a treat to meet the kids. Thank you for making the covers something special for my readers.

ABOUT THE AUTHOR

Miralee Ferrell, the author of the Horses and Friends series plus fifteen other novels, was always an avid reader. She started collecting first edition Zane Grey Westerns as a young teen. But she never felt the desire to write books . . . until after she turned fifty. Inspired by Zane Grey and old Western movies, she decided to write stories set in the Old West, in the 1880s.

After she wrote her first novel, *Love Finds You in Last Chance, California,* she was hooked. Her *Love Finds You in Sundance, WY,* won the Will Rogers Medallion Award for Western Fiction, and a TV production company has an option on 3 of her other books for possible movies.

Miralee loves horseback riding on the wooded trails near her home with her married daughter, who lives nearby, and spending time with her grandbaby, Kate. Besides her horse friends, she's owned cats, dogs (a seven-pound, long-haired Chihuahua named Lacey was often curled up on her lap as she wrote this book), rabbits, chickens, and even two cougars, Spunky and Sierra, rescued from breeders who couldn't care for them properly.

Miralee would love to hear from you:
www.miraleeferrell.com
www.twitter.com/miraleeferrell
www.facebook.com/groups/82316202888

BOOKS BY MIRALEE FERRELL

Horses and Friends—Middle Grade Books
A Horse for Kate
Silver Spurs
Mystery Rider
Blue Ribbon Trail Ride
Rebel Horse Rescue
Trouble on the Trail
(Releasing late Spring 2017)

Love Blossoms in Oregon Series
Blowing on Dandelions
Forget Me Not
Wishing on Buttercups
Dreaming on Daisies

Novella Collections
In Love and War
Heart of a Cowboy
The Cowboy's Bride
The Nativity Bride
Part of the Twelve Brides of Christmas collection
The Dogwood Blossom Bride
Part of the Twelve Brides of Summer collection

Love Finds You Series
Finding Love in Bridal Veil, Oregon
(Previously published as Love Finds You in Bridal Veil,
Oregon)
Love Finds You in Sundance, Wyoming
(Reprinted as Outlaw Angel)
Finding Love in Last Chance, California
(Previously published as Love Finds You in Last Chance,
California)
Finding Love in Tombstone, Arizona
(Previously published as Love Finds You in Tombstone,
Arizona)
(Sequel to *Love Finds You in Last Chance, California*)

Contemporary Women's Fiction
The Other Daughter
Finding Jeena
(Sequel to *The Other Daughter*)

Other Contributions/Compilations
A Cup of Comfort for Cat Lovers

Fighting Fear: Winning the War at Home

Faith & Finances: In God We Trust
Faith & Family: Daily Family Devotion

CPSIA information can be obtained
at www.ICGtesting.com
Printed in the USA
FSOW04n2111211217
42657FS